Parachute Girls

Jenny Hammerle

D1557137

***

For Betty, Kathy, Pat, & Colleen-

Thank you for trusting me with

Grandma's story.

Prologue

October 8, 1940

Manchester, England

The droning sound of aeroplane engines woke Kay from a sound sleep. She lay quietly awaiting the sirens she knew were soon to follow. The Blitz was nearly an everyday occurrence in Manchester over these last six weeks. While there was damage and the Luftwaffe was making a good attempt at targeting the industrial centre at the heart of her English town, they were unsuccessful at dampening the citizens' hearty spirit. Kay counted backwards in her head knowing she had little more than ten seconds before the sirens would begin.

She was fairly precise in her ability to gauge the proximity of the large bombers heading their way. It became a nightly challenge for her. Being only sixteen years old, the war made her nervous, but her sense of pride and stubbornness created in her a false bravado. Hitler's attempt to use nighttime raids as opposed to daytime ones to create widespread fear and pandemonium only strengthened her resilience.

"Ten, nine, eight."

"Kay! Get up! We must get down to the cellar!" Her youngest brother Anthony sounded from across the room in the darkness.

"Shh. Listen Anthony. Four, three, two, one." On cue the sirens blared through the sleepy streets. Kay sprang out of bed and ran across the room grabbing Anthony's outstretched hand. They sprinted downstairs, through the kitchen and towards the basement door. The first of many bombers flew just overhead. The German pilots made a habit of flying as low as possible, searching for targets, taunting the terrified British civilians as they passed. During the last several weeks Kay saw them pass so dangerously close, she could read the inscriptions on their wings. From the sound of it, tonight was no different.

She and Anthony entered the cellar and ran down the final flight of stairs.

"It's about time, Katie ." Her mother's hoarse, dry voice echoed in the cellar's dank darkness.

"I'm sorry, Mum. I didn't mean to frighten you."

"It's a dangerous game you're playing."

Kay walked over to her mother's makeshift cot in the corner of the cellar where her mother lay wrapped in blankets. Her head was propped up on pillows. Her mother's bouts with gall stones and catarrh made it necessary to move her bed to the basement. For months she'd been plagued with fever and vomiting. The doctor said not much could be done and keeping her comfortable was the best practise. Since the Blitz began weeks ago, Kay and Anthony lamented the relocation of their mother to the cellar. It couldn't be good for her lungs- the constant chill was distressing but she was not well enough to rush downstairs during the nightly bombings. So each day they would assist her as she gingerly made her way to the sitting room on the first floor, and each evening they'd assist her back down to the cellar. The cellar was quite cool tonight. Kay worried the worsening cold and dampness of the English winter would soon be upon them and would make it impossible for her mother to be down here, but winter was another three weeks away and she would have to make other arrangements then.

Kay went over to her mother and felt her head. Her forehead was a little damp, as well as her hair, where it stuck to her brow in moist clumps.

"I'm fine, my dear. I'm getting along well." Her mother lied up into her soft blue eyes.

"Yes, Mum."

Anthony came over and climbed into bed next to his mother and gave her a cuddle. Anthony was the last of the boys at home. The others volunteered to serve Jolly Old England. There were five of them in all. The four eldest weren't yet married, and as the list of casualties grew, Kay wondered if they ever would.

Why did this bloody war ever have to begin and why did my poor father have to die?

The ground quaked beneath Kay's feet as the bombs hit their targets- mostly factories and docks. It became a common sight in the Manchester city centre. A few smoldering buildings were usually visible at dawn, where the firemen worked tirelessly to dowse the flames, but in the end the bombs usually won out. The remnants of a large building would be nothing more than a hollowed out skeleton. Manchester's air raids hadn't been the all-out assault of the other major European cities, but even so…Kay feared the worst was yet to come.

Chapter One

Winter Haven, Florida

Present Day

"Happy Birthday dear Christine, Happy Birthday to you!"

The chorus of voices bellowed thunderously throughout the small dining room. Her grandmother's lilting English voice could be heard sweetly among the other raspier, less melodic pitches.

Christine blew out the twenty-five candles ablaze on her cake.

"Did you make a wish?" Her grandmother asked sweetly.

"I did and I'll share with you what I wished for."

"I don't know if sharing your wish is such a good idea. Not

that I buy into all of this foolish nonsense about if you share a wish, it won't come true and all. Some things though…are not meant to be shared. Some things should be kept just for you." Grandma explained as she sliced into the homemade yellow cake with strawberry cream cheese icing.

"Grandma's right. You shouldn't share your wishes." Connie, Christine's mother, added.

"I guess."

Christine stuck her fork into her wedge of cake and popped the large bite into her mouth.

"If you keep eating like this you won't fit into your bridal gown in six months." Her mother warned.

"Pity there."

While Christine mumbled the last part under her breath, she knew from her grandmother's sideways glance she'd caught her slip up. They visited for a while longer and then her mother, Uncle Tom, and Aunt Teri said their goodbyes. Christine decided to stay after the others departed and visit with her grandmother a few hours longer. Since graduating college and taking a full time job, she didn't get over as often as she used to.

She went into the kitchen where she helped Grandma wash the dishes by hand. Even though her grandmother owned a dishwasher she refused to use the thing claiming the old-fashioned way was still best at getting dishes clean. Christine worked in silence washing everything in sight until she had dishpan hands. Her grandmother cleared away the last of the plates and placed the remaining cake on her cake plate, wrapping it tightly in plastic wrap. She took a seat at the kitchen window and sipped her tea enjoying its strong, smooth taste.

"Grandma?"

"Yes."

"Were you scared to get married?"

"Scared? Oh course. I think all women are. Why?"

"I think I'm a little reluctant."

"I sensed that earlier. Is your reluctance what all the wish business was about?"

"Yes, and the fact that Jeffrey and I are fighting over wedding stuff."

"Come sit and talk with me- but put the kettle on first. I have a feeling this is more of a pot of tea conversation rather than a cuppa conversation."

Christine placed the dish towel on the front of the stove where it could dry. She put the kettle on the front burner and turned it to high. She took a seat with her grandmother at the small dinette.

"So you're nervous about getting married?"

"I am. I wasn't when I said yes."

"No- that's the easy part. The getting married and staying married is the hard part of the whole lot."

"I'm glad I'm not the only one to feel this way."

"Of course not. They don't call it cold feet for nothing. I felt just the same when I married your grandfather."

"You did?"

"I did. I was scared. He was a Yank and I a British girl. Our backgrounds were so different- he and his ways were foreign to me- but in the end it all worked out pleasantly."

"There are so many unknowns. I wonder if Jeff and I will be happy. Will we have children? Will we live here around family? He is from Illinois. Will he want to pick up and move there to be closer to his family at some point?"

"These are all things you need to discuss, but I think the

really important question here is whether or not any of those things would be a game changer for you."

Her grandmother looked at her over the rim of her tea cup. Christine thought about it long and hard before speaking again.

"I guess you're right. None of those things would be a 'game changer'. I want children and a move to Illinois wouldn't be the end of the world and all."

"Then, there's your answer. The more important thing here is the commonalities you and Jeff share. Your values and views on marriage, religion, child rearing- even politics. You don't have to be an exact replica of each other- in fact it would make things quite dull. All in all, those are the things you should discuss and come to some sort of agreement on. The rest will sort of work itself out."

"Thank you Grandma. You've just made my wish come true. You've put me at ease."

"Good. Wishes. Hmm. Now that's something I haven't thought about in a long time."

"Well, you do have a birthday coming up- perhaps it's time for you to come up with some new wishes."

"It wouldn't take much for me to come up with one. I've

honestly been thinking on something for quite a while. Perhaps you could help me with it."

"I'd love to. Tell me what it is and we'll make it happen."

"I'd like to go back."

"Go back? To England?"

"To England- one last time."

"It doesn't have to be the last time Grandma. You're still young. You're only turning seventy-eight."

"Spoken like the youth you are my dear. No- I'm still young. I'm young enough to visit everyone and see the things I want to see, do the things I want to do and share those experiences with you. In another ten years I may not be well enough to do it. Going home one last time would be my wish."

"Then, we'll do it. You've gone with Mama and then with Carol- now it's my turn."

"Something like this will take planning- are you sure you're up to it?"

"Leave it to me- of course Mama may want to join us, too."

"She may."

Christine and her grandmother visited for another ten

minutes. Afterwards Christine drove home and immediately set to work outlining the details of their trip. Her grandmother was from England, somewhere in Lancashire- apart from this she knew little else. In all the time she'd spent with her grandmother she realised they'd never discussed the details of her grandmother's life overseas- not really discussed it. Her childhood, her friends, her family and wartime England were largely a mystery to Christine.

Her grandmother was a devout Catholic, walking to mass everyday of her life- rain or shine. She worked her entire life running a school cafeteria in south Broward County near Ft. Lauderdale. She was a British war bride who came to the United States sometime after World War II following her marriage to an American GI. Beyond this, their relationship and history was unknown. It's not like grandma kept it a secret- maybe Christine never asked.

Christine contemplated the life her grandmother lived. She considered her grandmother's earlier comments about her age and health. Her desire to see England *one more time*...Christine became acutely aware her time to learn more of her grandma's story, first hand, was running out. Would she regret not knowing the details of her life better? The more she thought about it, the more she knew the answer to her question was yes. She dialled her mother.

"Hey, it's me Chris. I want to go to England- with Grandma."

"This is rather sudden. What brought on this immediate urge to travel?"

"Well- you've been."

"Yes. I went and took my mother when I was eighteen. It was the trip of a lifetime."

"Carol's been."

"That was her graduation gift from high school. We offered to do the same for you but you declined saying you were fearful of travelling abroad."

"Yes. Well, that's changed. I'm getting married in the spring. I'll be starting a family at some point after that. There may not be another opportunity for me to go. I want to take Grandma- for her birthday in September. She said she wished to see it all again one last time and I just added it to my leap list."

"Is the leap list something along the lines of the bucket list?"

"No, it's totally different. The bucket list is the list of things to do before you die- or kick the bucket- hence the name bucket list. The leap list is the list of things to do before you get married- or make the leap. So priority number one on my leap list is go to England!"

"I never had a leap list."

"It didn't exist then."

"Ok. Then we'll make it happen. But your timing only gives us three months to plan."

"I'm pulling up flights as we speak. Where do we fly in?"

"Manchester."

"How long should we visit?"

"Two weeks."

"Okay. I'll find the least expensive flights leaving around the time of Grandma's birthday and returning two weeks later. What about hotels?"

"We'll stay with family. It would insult them if we did otherwise."

"Okay."

"Let me know the cost. We'll split it."

Christine disconnected the call. Within minutes she'd booked the two week holiday. When she finalised her purchase an enormous feeling of elation washed over her. Christine's sister, Carol, studied abroad in three countries in addition to travelling all over Europe. Christine was always a little more reluctant to do anything outside her own home state, let alone outside the country. Even for college she'd insisted on selecting a school a mere two and a half hours from home. She'd never really severed the apron strings. She made routine visits home and even still went on holiday with her parents. Her wedding was just around the corner and while she lived on her own- she'd never really ventured out on her own. This trip with her grandmother was one she wanted more than she'd initially anticipated.

Over the next couple of weeks, Connie took care of notifying their British relatives of their coming visit. They were elated. It had been almost ten years since her grandmother's last visit with Carol and over thirty years since her visit with Connie. The family still remained quite close through the years regardless of distance and time. While Grandma only ventured over there twice in the last thirty years, her British relatives visited the United States a dozen or so times over the past three decades. Her grandmother's one brother, Anthony, still lived. Christine was certain his age and health was one of the most obvious reasons for this visit.

After weeks of planning, shopping and packing, the day finally came for their departure. It was autumn in Florida, but the heat wave and resulting high temperatures made it feel more like an endless summer. Christine, Connie and Kay dressed in layers recognising while it was warm in Florida it would be cool in Manchester. Christine picked her grandmother up at two o'clock in the afternoon accompanied by her sister and mother. Her sister wouldn't be going on this trip. Carol was now a mother of two with a third baby on the way. Christine could tell it pained her not to be able to partake in their adventure, but promised to bring her something special upon her return. Today Carol's role would be that of chauffeur. She'd drive the three of them to the airport and see them off. Then she'd go home only to return two weeks later to fetch them home again.

Grandma was very nicely dressed in a pair of slacks and a matching jacket. They were a soft shade of pink which cast a rosy glow on her cheeks. Kay had taken the time to curl her hair and apply make up. Christine couldn't remember a time when her grandmother wasn't properly *turned out*, as she called it. Even at seventy-eight she took pride in her appearance. She was one of the few women still in existence who believed your lip and nail colour should always match. Painted nails were a necessity- no true lady left the house otherwise!

On their way to the airport, Connie checked all of their paperwork, passports, drivers' licences, and boarding passes one final time making sure everything was in order. Over their arms each one carried a lightweight jacket. Christine checked the weather and saw it was raining and cold. She brought along a colourful muffler tied around her neck. It was a gift given to her by Jeff just this morning. While currently it was causing her to break out in a sweat, she knew she'd be thankful she'd brought it in about twelve hours. She would stow it as soon as she was comfortably seated onboard the plane.

When they arrived at the airport, they proceeded to their gate and awaited their boarding call. The moment finally arrived. Goodbye hugs were exchanged and a teary eyed Carol waved as they entered the gate leading through the security check and to their plane. Onboard the giant, jumbo aeroplane, the staff was courteous and upbeat- all of them British. Grandma took a seat next to Christine and patted her knee.

"It's a long flight. Do you think you'll be able to sleep at all?"

"I doubt it." Christine commented.

"Good. I've never been able to sleep on an aeroplane either. It'll give us time to chat."

Her grandmother fastened her seatbelt for take off. The remaining passengers boarded the plane. When the flight stewardess called for everyone to buckle their seatbelts, Christine could feel the jet begin its taxi towards the runway. The stewardesses went over the safety brochure and emergency exits. Christine's palms were sweating profusely. While she'd never vocalised it, she was not a happy flyer. She hated aeroplanes and being in the air. She closed her eyes and breathed quietly.

"Your grandfather loved to fly."

"That gene certainly bypassed me."

Her grandmother laughed softly.

"Me too- unless of course it was with him. I used to fear flying. Then he took me up with him and showed me the cockpit. He explained the true nature of flight- the physics of it. I fell in love with flying that day and haven't feared it since."

Moments later they lifted off and were climbing slowly into the sky. It was early evening and Christine knew with the time difference and the ten hour flight, they were scheduled to land sometime around five o'clock in the morning. On cue her grandmother jumped into conversation working to ease Christine's nerves.

Chapter Two

October 1940

Manchester, England

As the hours passed and the sounds of bombs faded into the night, Kay left the cellar leaving both her mother and brother sleeping down below. Upstairs she put on the kettle for tea and made breakfast of heavy cakes sans butter or pudding. Things like butter, milk, eggs, meat and most fruits were nearly impossible to get. Rationing made cooking more challenging and this morning's feast was no exception. The cakes were flat and heavy, but would have to do. Since Kay's father died over a year ago, she'd made the decision to take a job at a pastry shop where she learned to bake meat pies. These days there wasn't a market for meat pies or any meat to put in them. As a result her job in the pastry shop was short lived and she'd had to find other employment. At home her weekly ration of horse meat was all she had for meat- at least the pastry dough and gravy she used in the pasties made them edible.

One by one her brothers were called into service starting with Jimmy and ending with George. They were now stationed all over England, and one- as far away- as Scotland. They wrote her every now and again and she wrote back. Anthony was but thirteen years and Kay was hopeful by the time he achieved nineteen years the war would've ended. All young men were called to serve at nineteen years and most were glad to do so. The war had already taken Jimmy, Billy, George, and Jonathan away from her temporarily. Would it steal young Anthony too?

The sun crested the shoals in the North and Kay set the table for breakfast. For other sixteen year olds, getting up at two o'clock in the morning and staying awake all night to the sounds of bombing in the nearby distance, only to go to work for the day, would be odd. But not for her. She made her way back down to the cellar and assisted her mother upstairs, her on one side and Anthony on the other. They sat her in the rocking chair next to the fireplace where Kay rekindled last night's coals and quickly built a warm, blazing fire.

"Thank you, Katie . It feels so nice." Her mother coughed into her handkerchief and wiped her mouth. She spat something into it Kay couldn't see.

"Mum- are you well?"

"A little under the weather this morning is all- nothing to be bothered about."

Though Kay knew her mother was lying to her, she saw little other choice than to go to work and continue her day. Her brothers, all being single, would receive service pay. She expected it to arrive at the house on a monthly basis, but the process was a slow one and as of today Kay had only received one payment. So like so many others, she set off to her job hopeful the war would end and things would soon return to normal. She carried her mother's breakfast tray over to her and placed it on her lap.

"Can I bring you anything else Mum before I head out?"

"No, Dear. Anthony will assist me with anything I need.

Have a safe and blessed day."

"Yes, Mum I will try. Harry has been tireless lately. Since there isn't a market for men's dress trousers he has changed our roles. For three weeks now I've been stitching men's military slacks. I like it. At least I'm doing my part. Maybe a pair of my slacks will find their way to Jimmy."

"What a sweet thought, maybe they will."

Kay bent and kissed her mother goodbye. She hugged Anthony and walked out onto Plymouth Street. A glance beyond her street told her all she needed to know about last night's Blitz. The military targets near the docks were hit. The cotton factory levelled and taken out. Plumes of black smoke rose into the morning sky. Her only relief was the factory would have been closed and the loss of life therefore limited, if any. Kay made her way to the corner and caught the bus which would carry her to the heart of the shopping district and the tailor shop where she worked. The buses were used by civilian workers commuting during the daytime hours, but by four o'clock they were reserved for military use. Harry rearranged their schedules weeks ago, making it so they could arrive home before that time. The change to her schedule was about the only welcomed change the war brought about.

She arrived a little before eight o'clock, where Constance stood waiting outside.

"Harry's not here yet?"

"Hardly. That man never misses a day of work! He'd be here even if it meant burying his mother on the way first!"

Kay giggled and slapped Constance's wrist.

"Stop it, Constance . He is a good and kind man. I for one am glad to have this job and the wages, too. Without it I don't know where I'd be. Mum is doing poorly though she'll hardly admit it. I'm afraid I may have to admit her to hospital shortly."

"I hope not. I was waiting for you actually."

"Okay, but let's go inside. You know how Harry feels about idleness."

The two girls walked into the shop. Harry greeted them from behind the till and nodded at the girls, pointing to the large bolts of fabric stacked in the corner nearby.

"Girls- we have received a large order from the British Royal Guard. We need to produce as many pairs of trousers as possible. I'm upping your normal quota from ten a day to fifteen."

Both girls' eyes widened to the size of saucers.

"I know it's daunting but you can do it. Now get to work."

Kay and Constance set to work on their large sewing machines. Each machine housed a double needle and was quite dangerous. The material was thick and heavy, made to withstand days, weeks or even months of wear with little to no mending. Though their shift wasn't scheduled to begin for another fifteen minutes the girls began work straight away knowing there was no time to lose. Harry, while a task master, was an honest man. He always insisted on paying the girls top wage, as well as any overtime they might have earned. As far as bosses went, he was a good one. Within minutes Veronica, Hilda, and Theresa arrived.

"What's the hurry, girls?"

"Harry's given us a new project. Trousers for the British Royal Guard. Get sewing. There is a sheet at each of our work stations detailing the pant sizes. I have the trousers for the short and rotund." Constance joked about the thirty-eight inch waist and twenty-eight inch inseam pair of slacks she was currently stitching on her machine. "Kay there is the lucky one. She is stitching the slacks for the tall, fit, and devastatingly good looking gentlemen."

"What size are hers?"

"Thirty-three inch waist and thirty-six inch inseam."

The girls all whistled in response to her detailing of the trousers she sewed.

"Mine aren't so bad!" Theresa called from her machine. "I'm to sew thirty inch waist and thirty-two inch inseam. Average height and fairly fit."

"Ladies, let's remember regardless of shape these gentlemen are serving England." Hilda held up a pair of enormous trousers. All of the women roared with laughter.

"Are you sure you've sewn those correctly?"

"Of course, I'm sure. It says right here: Twenty pairs of thirty-six by thirty-six."

"If you say so. That is one big bloke!"

"I wouldn't mind meeting him and a few of his mates as well." Veronica muttered under her breath. When all of the other girls just gaped at her she added. "What? I like a lot of man."

"Or a giant!"

"Why not?"

"I have an idea." Constance announced as she cut another

few yards of fabric from a large bolt.

"This should be good." Kay teased.

"Okay, poke fun if you want but I'm serious. I think we should write a handwritten note and tuck it into the pocket of each pair of trousers. A thank you note. Then when the men receive these it will brighten their day to know they were sewn with thought and consideration by a group of women who truly cared."

"Works for me."

"Enough chatter, ladies. More sewing." Harry called as he made his way back to the stockroom.

The girls sewed for the next several hours breaking only for a cup of tea and scones around lunch time. All of them were youthful- Kay at sixteen was the youngest. Theresa and Constance were both eighteen while Veronica was nineteen. While Hilda at twenty-one was the most senior in both age and work experience, she seemed to the others to be nearly forty and was really more matronly. She was married and had a baby on the way. She was due sometime in the spring. Her husband worked in some capacity at hospital in theatre. Theatre was the area of hospital where surgeries were performed. Kay knew little else of Hilda's husband or private life. She always kept it this way. Private. Hilda spoke with an Austrian accent and since the war began she never discussed the Germans or anything else for that matter. She was loyal to the British, having married an Englishman and that was that.

Veronica was the only child of the Hodges who owned a bakery in Manchester. She met Kay when she worked at the pasty shop next door and when Kay came to work for Harry, Veronica came along as well. Veronica's parents were more than happy for her to learn a new trade. There was always work available to seamstresses and now with the food shortages and rations, her parents' bakery wasn't the thriving business it once had been. As a result, Veronica's wages from Harry were what they depended on to make ends meet.

Theresa was the oldest of six daughters. Her father was a hardworking man employed in the cotton textiles near the Picadilly. Her mother stayed home with four of the younger daughters who were still in school at St. Mary's Girls' School in Manchester. Theresa's fourteen year old sister, Elizabeth, would complete her Christmas term shortly and having achieved fourteen years would be eligible for completion to enter into a trade or employment. Theresa had already taught her to sew at home. Therefore, Harry had made her a promise of employment here at the shop.

Constance was Kay's closest and dearest friend. At two years her senior, she was more like the older sister Kay had never had than a friend. Constance's parents were elderly and quite frail. She lived alone with them as their full time nurse and helpmate. Her one and only brother married a French girl ten years earlier and lived in Paris. Since the war and the subsequent attacks in Paris had begun, correspondence from him was few and far between. Last she knew he was alive and well. That was before the invasion and surrender in June. His wife died in a bombing earlier this year. He was working for a bank at the time and beyond this Constance knew nothing of his whereabouts or well-being.

Through doubt and uncertainty about her brother, Constance had born it well. All four of Kay's older brothers were away but she knew where they were and their letters served as a reminder all was not lost. By three o'clock the girls called it a day, said their goodbyes, and made their way out to the corner to wait for their buses.

At home Anthony had already started dinner. Fish and chips

became the daily fare at their home. Aside from the horse meat, fish was the only other source of protein available. The cycle was only broken by the occasional meat pie, or beans on toast, and jam butties. Kay longed for fresh fruit- a banana- or perhaps a green vegetable of some sort. Potatoes, rhubarbs, red currants, and apples were the only fresh produce available from a small garden their house shared with Martha, her neighbour to one side, and she was tired of eating them. Potatoes- mashed, boiled, baked or fried. It was chips with everything. As Kay arrived home it was no different than any other day. They listened to the radio for any news of the war, anything at all which might bring them word about her brothers. Most times there was nothing. They finished dinner after which her brother and she escorted their mother back down to the cellar. Her mother was growing increasingly feeble and while Kay knew a cellar was not the best location for her, she knew they didn't have much other choice. She prayed this would soon change.

This evening her mother seemed exceptionally tired. Kay and Anthony decided to move a single sized mattress downstairs as well. The stairwell was narrow and it would take some manoeuvering but working together they could manage. By nine o'clock and well past dark, Kay fashioned the single mattress into a comfortable bed on the floor. It was far softer than the cot. Anthony and Kay slept one at either end, each sharing only a corner of the mattress for his head and neck until nearly three o'clock in the morning when the next round of air raids began.

This morning's air raids seemed much closer than the others had been. The ack-ack guns and incendiary bombs were deafening. Their home was located on Plymouth Street and was a fair distance from the usual targets. With each bomb sounding nearer and nearer, Kay could hear her mum praying in her bed nearby. She was holding her rosary merely asking the Lord to show mercy. Kay left her brother sleeping on the cot they'd moved to in the middle of the night and went to sit with her mother.

"How far we have come that he can actually sleep through this noise?" Her mother pondered.

"Yes, I wonder at it myself. He must be quite exhausted."

Bessie coughed loudly into her handkerchief and covered her mouth. There was a deep rattling in her lungs where none existed before. The handkerchief was stained red.

"Don't be alarmed." Bessie reached over patting Kay's hand.

"Mum- I think we need to move you to hospital where you can receive proper care."

"I agree." Bessie paused looking over to where Anthony lay sleeping. "What about your brother? With you working every day, and gone most of the time, I'm fearful he will be so lonely."

"He is finished with school now. He is supposed to enter into a trade. Perhaps if I speak with someone we can find him something to occupy his time."

"Perhaps. Promise me no matter what happens you will look after him. Your brothers are grown Katie and you're a woman now. Promise me."

"I promise, Mum."

Kay covered her mother and lay down beside her holding her hand. The bombs quieted and the sirens stopped. They slept until dawn. She rang the shop and spoke with Harry in a hushed whisper advising him she needed to take her mother to hospital. Harry understood and told her to take the day. While she was appreciative of the gesture, Kay could hardly afford to miss an entire day's wages. It would put her behind on her quota and she knew better than to think she would be able to make it up.

She packed her mother a small carrying case of what little toiletries she possessed, as well as a change of clothing. She closed the case and heard the bell of the front door. She wasn't expecting company and came running when she heard Anthony's squeals of delight.

Kay stopped cold at the sight of George standing in the small kitchen. He was serving in the Signal Corps where he worked on the search lights. Kay ran and threw her arms around him. It had been nearly a year- ten months to be exact- since she had last seen him. George was the eldest of her five brothers at twenty-four years old. While he was thinner and somewhat pale, he was still tall and as handsome as always.

"What are you doing here?" Anthony stepped back to look him over. The initial joy he'd felt was surpassed by a new uneasiness and concern.

"I'm on furlough for an injury to my hand and foot. I received a burn and will be home for a month until I regain full use of both."

"While I'm sorry for the burn and pain you must be feeling, I can't say I'm sorry you're home. It's so good to see you George."

Kay threw her arms around her brother, giving him a squeeze.

Just having George home again warmed Kay's heart. He was a man and with his presence he brought a sense of stability and permanence which was missing since her father's death and the departure of all of her other brothers.

"Where's Mum?"

"That's just it. Anthony and I were just about to carry her to hospital. She has catarrh and has been suffering greatly with the gall stones and stomach ulcers. Now with this cough getting worse- I am becoming concerned. Anthony- do you mind running upstairs and grabbing her overnight case I packed. In my haste to see George I've gone and forgotten it upstairs."

Anthony disappeared up the steps taking two at a time.

"She is not well, George. She has been coughing up blood for the last few days. I only just learnt of it. I don't want Anthony to know."

"Of course not."

"Then, there is the fact she wants Anthony to find employment. She is afraid he will become depressed and lonesome with all of us gone."

"It seems I'm home just in time. I can take care of this for you. Consider it handled. I will see to it he has a job before I leave."

Anthony appeared at the foot of the stairs.

"All set."

Kay and George went down into the cellar to fetch their mother.

"What a lovely surprise, George!" was all she could say between sobs and cuddles.

George picked her up and carried her upstairs and outside to await the bus.

"Katie - why don't you let us men attend to Mum? You go on to work."

"I'll be up to see you everyday, I promise." Kay bent and kissed her mother's hair.

"Of course, you will, my dear girl. Now run along." Her mother kissed her cheek.

Kay boarded the bus and paid her fare. She waved out the window to the three of them where they awaited the next bus which would carry them to Manchester where the hospital was located.

When Kay entered into the shop, Harry was there behind the

till as always.

"That took you much less time than I'd anticipated."

"Me, too. George came home."

At the announcement of George's sudden return home, Theresa's head shot around as if she'd been struck.

"George's home?"

"Just. He received some sort of burn to his hand and foot. He will be home for a month until he is healed."

"Burns can be nasty affairs." Hilda advised.

"Yes, but I didn't get to look at them. They're both bandaged- his hand and his foot."

"I've got some training in first aid. Maybe I should take a look." Theresa offered.

Hilda cut her eyes at Veronica and Constance .

"Maybe you should." Constance raised her eyebrows up and down. "Maybe he needs new trousers while you're at it."

All the women laughed at this suggestion.

"Maybe he does but this pair of thirty-two inch inseam certainly won't fit him. Kay - I'll be needing a pair of those."

"Don't hold your breath. Brother or not I need every pair for my quota today. If you're wanting a pair in his size you'll have to sew them yourself."

"I will. I have just the fabric at home. A lovely navy will be perfect for what I have in mind."

#

"Grandma?" Christine interrupted her grandmother's thoughts. "So during the war you were how old?"

"Just sixteen when it began."

"And your mother was sick?"

"She was quite poorly, yes."

"And Theresa was in love with George?"

"Yes. She always had been."

"And she sewed him pants?"

"Yes- we're getting to that part."

"I just can't imagine sewing Jeff a pair of pants- as a gift."

"Times were different. It was wartime England. We couldn't just run out and buy what we needed. Most times we made it."

"Wow. Continue. I'm sorry for interrupting."

Her grandmother lightly squeezed her hand before continuing.

Chapter Three

True to her word, Theresa rode the bus home with Kay to

check on George. She'd always thought George was handsome, and

though he was six years older than her, it made no difference. Even

the distance of the past year and wartime did little to diminish her

dreams of dating him. When they arrived at the gate to Kay's front

garden and opened it, the smell of dinner greeted them.

"Smells like an apple tart."

"George must be in the kitchen because there is no way

Anthony could manage an apple tart on his own."

Their mother, Bessie, was an incredible baker. She'd worked

in a bakery for years and trained Kay and her older sons to cook amazing treats. Times became difficult, and since she'd taken ill two years ago, poor Anthony's lessons were suspended. Shortly after, their father died unexpectedly one evening due to complications of stroke and paralyses of the nerves. Their mother's illness worsened and the untimely war began. A compilation of these seemed to all join forces. The end result was Kay working outside the home and Anthony barely managing to finish school. Kay so hoped George's sudden appearance home was a sign this sad chapter in their life would soon end and life would return to normalcy.

When Kay entered the kitchen, George was hard at work at the stove. He did a double take at Theresa standing in the doorway-obviously not expecting company for dinner.

"I brought a guest for dinner. I hope this is okay."

"Theresa is always welcome in our home. You look well Theresa."

His compliment made Theresa blush. She'd been but sixteen the last time he saw her. She'd always been a rather skinny teenager. All legs and teeth. Now she was eighteen. She'd really grown into an attractive young lady. Her long, lean frame was replaced by a more womanly figure. Her short bob grown to waist length, blonde hair. Her face was now more heart shaped than it was before. Her pointed chin appeared delicate in contrast to the youthful fullness of her cheeks. She had truly become pretty. Kay was sure her brother noticed the changes as well. George kept glancing at Theresa where she sat at the kitchen table sipping tea- as if he couldn't believe his eyes.

"How old are you now, Theresa?"

"Eighteen just last month."

"How are your parents and sisters?"

"They're all well, no complaints other than the war. Father's still working in the cotton textile. Mum's home with the girls. My sister, Elizabeth, is soon to start work with Kay and me."

"Sounds promising."

"Yes, I certainly hope so. The more of us working the better. I heard about your hand and foot. Do they bother you much?"

"Not really. My hand got the worst of it. I have some nerve damage, but I'm hoping in time it will fully recover."

Kay noticed how he was using his left hand rather than his right, careful not to bump the bandaged hand.

"I've some training in first aid and would help you bandage it if you'd allow me."

He shot Kay a glance. She wasn't sure if it was a look of 'is she serious' or of embarrassment. Kay didn't know how bad the burns really were- or if it could be scarred. Maybe he didn't want this pretty young lady seeing it. Maybe it shamed him. She couldn't be sure.

"Thanks for the offer, Theresa, but Kay will tend to it. It is a rather bad burn and I wouldn't want you to have to see it."

"I understand."

Kay smiled sweetly at Theresa. Theresa was always timid and awkward. While she was older than Kay, her shyness made her seem younger. Sensing this Kay decided to intervene and help her friend where her brother was concerned.

"Theresa thought since we are sewing trousers for the servicemen you might need a pair or two. She has some lovely navy material she has no use for and I thought it was a fantastic idea. What do you say?"

"I can't say I disagree. The ones I have are worn and beyond repair. I'm not sure if four weeks is enough time to sew them though."

"We weren't planning on doing them by hand." Theresa seized the opportunity to enter into the conversation. "Harry will allow us to use the machines at work, on our own time of course and after all of our other work is finished. It's the least we can do. Consider it a welcome home gift."

"Thank you. I accept. I'm a thirty-three thirty-six. I can't wait to try them on."

Anthony appeared in the doorway. He was washed and cleaned up. He wore his best slacks and a pale blue shirt. Kay knew instinctively it was in honour of their dinner guest. Even at fourteen Anthony recognised just how pretty Theresa had become. George just smiled over at Kay as he brought serving dishes to the table.

"After dinner I thought I might go up and see Mum." Kay took a bite of chip dipped in vinegar.

"I'd love to join you, but after standing on my foot all day I really need to get off it. Maybe Anthony will walk you."

Kay glanced at the amazing meal George had prepared. She realised that in order to have the egg and precious other supplies he'd prepared for supper, George must have gone to stand in the ration queue in town. Kay didn't have the time to do as such most days. She usually sent Anthony while she was at work. The lines were long, as well as the wait. A person could wait for hours only to receive a potato or two.

"I'd be happy to walk you." Anthony offered. "Did you want to come as well, Theresa?"

A hopeful Anthony beamed at her from across the table.

"I wish I could, but I better be getting home after dinner. Mum will be worried if I'm not home within the hour."

Anthony looked sullen.

"Perhaps I could see you home and pop in on your parents. It's not but a few blocks walk." George offered.

"That would be lovely."

Kay could see from the look on Anthony's face everyone thought so except for him. He looked downright angry. Sensing Anthony's mood, dinner conversation lagged a bit until Theresa asked George about his service. After dinner Theresa insisted on clearing the table while George rested his leg. Kay and Anthony made their way out of the house and down the lane passing the bus stop. It was a cool, clear evening and the walk was not all that far.

Neither of them minded the fresh evening air.

"She is too old for you."

"What difference does four years make? George is six years older than she. I'd say he is too old for her."

"Yes, well there is their age difference but she is eighteen. She is an adult, as is he. The right girl is out there for you- you just haven't met her yet."

Kay used the side of her foot to lightly kick her brother's backside. When he started to complain she just winked at him. They linked arms and walked the remaining distance to the hospital. The nurse at the desk pointed them to the third floor and informed them they would only have a short time to visit with their mother. Visiting hours ended at seven o'clock.

Their mother was snoring lightly when they entered the room. The gown she was wearing was clean and so was her room. On a tray beside her bed, there was broth and a small dinner roll. She had drunk most of the broth and had eaten all but one bite of the roll. Kay hadn't tasted a bite of fresh bread in over six months. Seeing it now set both her and Anthony's mouths to watering. There was a small container of jam next to it and they could see their mother used most of what she'd been given. Her colour already looked better.

"Mum." Kay lay her hand on her mother's arm. Her mother's eyes fluttered open.

"Hello, children. I'm so glad you came. I ate the most wonderful dinner and they've started me on antibiotic. I should be up and around in no time."

"Any news on the stones, Mum?"

"No, just the same. I must limit my movement and if I'm well enough I can have surgery to remove my gall bladder. In time it will all work out."

"Yes- of course, it will."

"How is George?"

"Right now he is walking Theresa home. She came by with me after work and stayed for dinner."

"That's nice, Dear. She has always harboured such a soft spot for George. Maybe now seeing as she is not all legs and elbows he'll pay her some attention."

Anthony just rolled his eyes. Kay elbowed him in the side.

"Anthony is a bit jealous."

"It's only natural that you should be jealous. Your turn will come. When the war ends there will be lots of young women in search of a young man. You'll see."

Katie brushed her mum's long beautiful, silver grey hair and then braided it over one shoulder. It seemed to relax her. It was one of her favourite things to do. In the last few years it was the one thing she still did to show the love and appreciation she felt for her mother. It required little time and no money or resources.

Anthony laid his head on Bessie's hospital bed while she stroked his hair and hummed a lullaby from their childhood. *Too-ra-loo-ra-loo-ra* was a family favourite passed down through generations. When she finished the Irish lullaby, Mum seemed very sleepy. Just then a nurse came in and handed her some pills along with a small cup of water.

"Visiting hours are over. You can come again tomorrow evening."

"Thank you. Good night, Mum."

"Good night and God bless."

Anthony and Kay walked the same way they'd come only an hour or so earlier. It was quickly approaching dusk and they leisurely strolled down the lane making their way towards home. They were nearly there when they heard the piercing sirens wailing in the distance. There had never been an air raid this early in the evening. Usually the German pilots saved their terrifying attacks for the dead of night- not dusk. Kay grabbed Anthony's hand and they ran.

They could hear the engines coming and soon a bomber flew directly overhead. The pilot flew so low Kay could see his goggles and read the writing on the wings of his plane.

Enmeshermits.

The Swastika was clearly visible. The first of the bombs fell all around them- they ran hoping to make it to their house and into the cellar. As they passed an open doorway, a man grabbed them both and pulled them onto the door stoop. He covered them with his body as they huddled together against a brick wall and locked door. The ground beneath their feet rumbled and shook. Kay thought the building might topple with the force of it all. The cacophony of guns, bombs, and sirens drowned out all thought and noise. They were thrown to the floor and flying debris showered them. When the rumbling stopped, and they opened their eyes, they met with utter devastation.

The man who shielded them lay upon Anthony, still holding

him though he was dead. Kay rolled his lifeless body off a terrified, grief stricken Anthony.

"Get up! We must get moving Anthony!"

Kay stood and saw the buildings which once stood on the street just minutes before were all levelled. The doorway they were in was all that remained. An injured dog wandered the street nearby confused and somewhat disoriented. She prayed a silent prayer of thanks to the stranger who had so bravely given his life to save her brother. She used her hand to close the stranger's eyes and covered him with her shawl.

A glance towards the direction of the hospital, where they just came from, frightened Kay for their mother's safety. The tall expanse of the hospital that usually lined the sky, among other tall buildings, was no more than a cloud of smoke. Black smoke tinged in orange spoke of an incredibly hot fire burning in the distance. Kay pulled Anthony with her as she ran the few blocks, returning to the site of the hospital, calling to their mother as they went. All that remained of the hospital wing was a hotly burning fire in a large crater…

Tears stung Kay's eyes and ran down her face. The hospital

should have been safe as it was clearly marked with a very large red cross on a white background on the roof. Violent sobs shook her chest and entire being. Anthony spoke not a word- nor made any sound. His eyes looked glassy and he was shaking.

In the distance, Kay could see more planes on the horizon and knew the second wave was coming. She grabbed Anthony's hand and began running once more. The streets were littered with debris- both large and small. An overturned bus, people rushing about and absolute chaos continued. This early evening attack took the citizens of Manchester by surprise.

This one would go down as a small victory for Hitler.

Kay pulled a shocked Anthony along behind her, jumping over small bricks and tree limbs. The smoke was dense making it difficult to breath. The sirens began again as they were a mere three blocks from home. The blocks leading up to their house were levelled with only a few row houses here and there left standing. As they rounded the corner and turned onto Plymouth, Kay breathed a sigh of relief to see their own house and the others on their street were left virtually untouched.

They sprinted up to the front gate and swung it open. Racing through the front door and down to the basement they found George and Theresa safely tucked away there. They secured the door and all held their breath as the bombs rained down an unceasing attack for more than four hours. As wave after wave came it was apparent this attack was different than the previous attacks had been. It came just a few days before Christmas.

The previous blitzes were all of a much shorter duration and seemed to target the war plants and factories key to the success of the British in World War II. This was different- very different. The following morning, in the light of day the catastrophic damage inflicted became all too apparent. Not only military targets but civilian targets were hit as well. Churches, hospitals and houses were all decimated. There seemed to be no limit to the cruelty of war.

Kay, Theresa, George, and Anthony made their way out the back door to inspect their home and neighbouring houses for damage. A huge hole greeted them where their garden once flourished, but their house sustained minimal damage. They checked on Martha next door. She too survived the blitz. A family down the end of their street hadn't been so lucky. Their home was gone and with it they all perished. Only their cat, Boots, walked around in the rubble, free from injury.

Kay picked him up and stroked his fur lovingly. He purred loudly and nuzzled up under her neck. She carried Boots back to her house and decided today would be the perfect time to add a pet to her life. Anthony and George made their way on foot into town to check on their mother. They were hoping that against all odds the patients had been evacuated to the hospital basement before the bomb hit.

Numb, Theresa walked home to her house a few blocks away. Luckily for her it was untouched and her family safe. Kay and her neighbour Martha set to work to try to right the wrecked garden. They found a few potato plants and rhubarb still clinging to life. The apple tree was gone as were the berry bushes.

"Take these, dear, and plant them in a small pot inside. It will be the safest way to garden over the next few weeks."

Martha handed her the precious plants. She went inside and reappeared with a few small pots. She scooped soil into the pots and carefully replanted the uprooted plants. Kay turned to go back inside when she saw Anthony and George coming out the backdoor. They must have just returned from hospital. She hoped they'd bring news of a miracle.

The looks on their faces confirmed what they all feared. Her mother's wing of the hospital sustained a direct hit. As a result all three floors were levelled. A mass grave was being dug; the remains of most were unidentifiable. Kay sank to her knees in the back alley upon hearing the news. George came over to her and carried her inside, upstairs to her room where he laid her on the bed, covering her with her mother's quilt. Anthony came to sit at the foot of her bed. All three sat and cried. A few moments later George stood and spoke determinedly.

"I'll write to the others and tell them of the Blitz- and Mum."

As the oldest it was George's place, and for this Kay was thankful. She knew she didn't have the strength to write to Jimmy, Billy, and Jonathan. She was relieved he did. Kay glanced over at Anthony who'd fallen asleep. He was so young and now he had lost both of his parents. Orphaned by war at fourteen, Kay was all he had left. She was his mother now- merely a child herself. She stood and covered him with her quilt and went downstairs to make dinner.

In honour of their mother, she made Yorkshire pudding with the last of the flour and eggs. She cut up the small amount of horse meat for a pie and added it to the remaining rhubarb. She seasoned it with some herbs she'd left drying in the kitchen window. She made a pot of weak tea and stepped back to see the meal she'd prepared. She knew her mother would've been pleased. She'd been a survivor. She wouldn't want Kay to cry- she wouldn't want her to mope. She would want her to be happy. She would expect her to be strong. Maybe Kay would be happy again. Some day- just not today.

"Where's Anthony?" George walked into the kitchen and took a seat.

"Resting upstairs."

"Good. I'll be home for another three weeks time. I'm healing nicely. Once I'm gone I've arranged for him to work at a factory in Trafford Park assembling engines and welding small parts. They're in need of women too. I thought you might want to pick up a few extra hours there as well."

"Of course."

The way George was forging ahead it seemed as if he was unaffected by their mother's death. Didn't he feel the loss as deeply as she did? If he did he didn't show it. He seemed put together as always.

"I've posted letters to Billy, Jonathan, and James. They should receive them within two weeks." A tear glinted in his eye, but remained unshed. He stood and pushed in his chair walking over to stand at the kitchen window and peering out at nothing. "Do me a favour Katie. Promise me once I leave you'll carry on. Straight to work and home again. No traipsing about, going to these dances and such. Yesterday was bad enough. We've lost Mum- it could've been worse. We could've lost you and Anthony as well. I think we need to start taking more precautions. Things are going to get a lot worse before they get better. I think the attacks of yesterday evening and last night were only the beginning. I wish I could stay behind with you both, but I can't. I have to rely on you to be strong. You're the woman of the house now."

Kay simply nodded her head when he turned to look at her. "Good."

Kay glanced at his bandaged hand and foot. They were filthy and hadn't been changed at all since his arrival as far as Kay knew.

"Have a seat. Let's see to those bandages."

George came over and did as she commanded. He removed his shirt and she was amazed to see the bandages went clear up to his shoulder and across the top of his chest. Her previous belief that only his hand and foot were affected was incorrect. She used her scissors to cut the bandages away. When the last of the bandages fell away she did her best not to gasp at what she saw.

"It's not as bad as it looks."

"How did this happen?"

"A search light makes an easy target. I suffered burns over most of my arm and chest, as well as my hip, leg and foot. Now you can understand why I wouldn't want Theresa to see such a thing. Wounds such as these would be haunting for her to see."

"I'm not so sure. I can understand you not feeling comfortable with her seeing them but I think she is made of tougher stuff than you think."

"She is the oldest of six girls, but I don't think she's doctored even a bloodied nose before."

"You like her don't you."

"I do."

"Well she likes you too."

"You don't say."

"Sure does. You should've seen the way her head snapped

around at hearing you'd come home. It was really her idea to make the trousers after all."

Then as soon as she spoke the words Kay wished she hadn't. What if her brother were no longer able to have children? She glanced at his leg wondering just how high his leg had been burned.

Catching her gaze, he winked over at her.

"Don't be alarmed- everything is still in good working order. My leg suffered the least damage and it was just that- only the leg and the top of the foot. It is my shoulder and arm that took the brunt of it."

"What about your partner- the other search light operator?"

"He wasn't as fortunate. I wrote to his wife and mother. War is a horrific thing, Kay. Do you remember the day when Jimmy heard about the war on the wireless radio? He and his friend Stephen raced home to tell us all the news. Of course we were all young lads then- foolish. We were dreamers with lofty ideas of war, about what it really was. We hadn't a clue. Not really. It's an ugly thing, Kay. A very, ugly thing."

"I know. Those who remembered the first World War knew how bad it could be- how bad it would be. I remember people rushing to get married- buying up the bridal gowns at pre-war sales. So many of those young lads are dead now." Kay paused examining her brother's wounds. "It looks like the worst of these has healed. It is only the minor ones which remain."

"I know. They wouldn't have let me travel otherwise- that and the fact they needed the bed."

"Well, I'm glad." Kay finished doctoring his chest and arm. George slipped his shirt back on and buttoned it. A light rap came at the door. Kay rose to answer it.

Big surprise- Theresa stood there a basket in hand.

"Come in, Theresa."

"Thank you, Kay. I heard about your mum. I'm sorry for your loss."

"Thank you. George and I just doctored his arm but have yet to do his leg."

"I won't be staying. Just needed to drop this for me mum." She handed the basket to George's outstretched hand.

"Smells delicious. What is it?"

"Scones but no jam I'm afraid. I helped."

"I'm sure they're wonderful."

Kay smiled at their polite exchange. Theresa seemed to be able to soften something in her brother's toughened demeanour. She brought out a gentler side of him. If Kay's own intuition didn't betray her, she suspected he liked her too- even more than he'd just admitted.

Kay walked Theresa outside. When she stepped back into the kitchen Anthony appeared from upstairs and sat eating scones.

"These are good."

"Better than good." George amended.

Kay walked over and tried one.

"They're fantastic. She's pretty and she cooks. You could do a lot worse George."

"Trying to marry me off little sister?"

"You're twenty-four."

"That I am. Let's get my leg doctored."

#

Kay stared out the aeroplane window- her mind lost in memories of war. A single tear trickled down her cheek. Christine now understood the reason for not sharing her life story before. As a child, hearing this tale would have scarred Christine. She couldn't imagine having to bare the loss of both of her parents, raising a teenaged brother and working- all the while facing the uncertainty of war. It seemed so unfair and harsh.

Christine's childhood was a happy one filled with trips to Disney World and weekends on the beach. Her biggest concern each day whether to do her homework before or after softball practise. She'd never been afraid of anything or anyone. She'd never feared bombings or starvation. She felt foolish for ever thinking her life difficult or tough.

Moments later her grandmother began again.

Chapter Four

"Whose idea were these notes again anyhow?" Veronica scribbled a note and hastily tucked it into the pocket of the trousers she'd just completed.

"I believe it was Constance's idea and I for one am enjoying writing the notes. I have four brothers serving Britain in some way or another. I like to imagine every pair of trousers goes to someone's brother, father, or son. In some small way I'm touching them."

"What are you writing?"

"Be safe and God Bless. Xoxo Kay. It's really that simple. I keep it the same for most of them- saying a small prayer over each one as I fold them and tuck the note safely inside."

"Okay- so that's where I was going amiss. I was writing a letter- as in a couple of paragraphs. I was beginning to wonder why it was taking me so much longer."

"Well, now you know, besides this is our last day sewing only men's slacks. As of tomorrow we're onto something new and very different." Hilda spoke between gritted teeth. She was in the process of replacing a broken needle on her machine.

"Don't leave us guessing Hilda. What is it?" Theresa came back from the stockroom with two new bolts of hunter green fabric.

"Parachutes. There is a military factory over in Stretford. They called Harry today- I overheard the conversation. They need help with parachutes."

"Harry volunteered us to sew parachutes?"

"Yes. We will still have pant orders to fulfill, but in between we will be sewing nylon parachutes."

"How do we put notes on those?" Theresa was replacing a huge bobbin of thread on her machine and rethreading her needles.

"On a small piece of paper pinned to the outside wrap." Constance offered cheerfully.

"I can't imagine how much fabric it will take to sew a

parachute, plus I'd imagine it isn't easy. Seems like it'd be challenging at the very least- slippery fabric. Sliding here and there- I can't say I'm excited about this new venture."

"Quit being so bleak about it, Veronica. You should be seeing it as your contribution to the war effort. Think of the men who'll use these parachutes."

"I hate this bloody war! I hate it! I hate the soldiers, the dying, and the suffering. The air raids- I hate the whole lot of it!"

"Veronica, don't say such things! Poor Kay's entire family has been affected by it and she is still positive." Theresa chided.

"No, she's allowed to express her disdain for the war- the violence, the suffering. I hate those things too, but not the soldiers. You should be thanking them Veronica- because of them we have not been invaded. Because of them you're still free." Kay touted.

Hilda stood and stalked over to where Veronica sat. She leaned over and spoke in a hushed tone.

"You're no more than a spoilt child. An only child who never had to work all that hard. Now you find yourself sewing for wages and actually having to earn your own way in life. Life is not fair. When you've lost your home, your family and all you hold dear then you can complain- until then shut your bloody mouth!"

With Hilda's order everyone worked in utter silence until it was time to leave. It was nearing the end of their shift when Harry came in.

"I don't think I've ever seen you all this focused. I assume we all know about the parachutes project."

Everyone nodded in unison, but no one spoke.

"Great. It won't be easy. The material may prove challenging at first but we can do it. Theresa's younger sister Elizabeth will be starting work tomorrow. Let's make her feel welcome. If there is nothing else have a safe trip home ladies."

Kay rose and pushed in her chair. Constance and Theresa came over to where she stood folding the last pair of trousers. Veronica passed by her work station on her way out.

"I apologise for my earlier remarks on the soldiers. I'm sorry."

"I'm not bothered, Veronica. We all have our own opinions."

"I should never have said it and I'm sorry."

"Apology accepted."

Kay strolled out onto the street corner. Since the Christmas

Blitz just weeks prior, the intensity of the raids just kept on increasing. The girls all knew they would have just a few precious hours to get home, cook, and get some sleep before the onslaught began again. Small posters and signs were nailed onto telephone poles and hung on doors. *Is that all you've got? We're still standing!* Flyers greeted them at every turn. The proud citizens of Manchester and its surrounding communities refused to give in to the German propaganda and bullying. The tenacity of the British spirit and steadfast resolve to persevere brought out the fighting side in every citizen. Bravely they worked day after day, tirelessly supporting the war effort.

Both Constance and Theresa became regulars in Kay's household these past several weeks. For Theresa the reason was clear- she and George began dating. Now he was preparing to depart just when they'd been getting on so well. They were spending every possible moment together. Her mother and her four youngest sisters had evacuated to the countryside, as was common for most school aged children. Only Theresa and Elizabeth remained behind with their father. All three would need to remain in town to work and provide for the family, while the small children sought safety in the country where bombings would be less likely.

For Constance the reasons for her frequent visits were different. She still hadn't heard anything about her own brother and her only companions at home were her parents. Both in their nineties, they remembered World War I and its devastating effects. Every night throughout the Luftwaffe they insisted Constance don and sleep in a fitted gas mask. Constance was positive the mask was giving her wrinkles at an early age- forcing her face into an unnatural shape. She would hide out at Kay's house until seven o'clock and then head home to tend to her duties there.

The bus pulled up to the corner. Lost in thought Kay didn't notice its appearance until Constance tugged on her shirt sleeve. On the bus ride home she started chatting about dating- or the lack thereof.

"I would just like to do something exciting- something other than sew trousers or parachutes. The only reason Theresa is so pleasant is she at least has someone."

"For now. He'll be leaving next week." Theresa moaned.

"Still, Kay and I haven't even dated. I can't even name an eligible man, other than Harry and he doesn't count because he is old enough to be our father!"

"That he is- but a handsome one at that." Theresa offered.

"I think he is younger than you both realise. Mid-thirties...maybe forty." Kay corrected.

"You know you're desperate when you find yourself ogling a sixteen year old only to find he is way too young for you!" Constance offered staring at a young man through her window, walking on the pavement, as they passed.

"You're only eighteen Constance and what sixteen year old were you eying?" Kay chided.

"Soon to be nineteen. All the men my age are off fighting. The ones here are either old or married or both. The sixteen year old was walking down my lane- I thought well there's one with a firm backside who's not taken- then he turned around. I could've fainted on the spot!"

"The war will be over soon enough."

The bus stopped at the end of Kay's street. They grabbed their totes and jumpers. There was a slight nip on the night air and Kay wrapped her jumper around her shoulders. Since the women and small children evacuated the city weeks ago, the streets became increasingly quiet. Between the bombed out houses and vacant lots where homes once stood, Kay's neighbourhood quickly became a ghost town. Only the old or working remained. Perhaps Constance was right.

"We're home, George."

"He's out." Anthony called from down the hallway. "Be back in a bit."

"Where'd he go?"

"To talk to Theresa's father. Said he had something important to ask." Anthony was looking very much like he knew a secret he had no intention of sharing- not realizing he'd just slipped up and told.

"Something you want to tell us?" Constance walked into the kitchen and plucked a recently washed apple off the counter.

"Don't look at me." Kay walked over and grabbed one as well.

"I better be going. See you both tomorrow."

Theresa excused herself without another word and skipped from the house.

"They getting married?"

"I'm guessing. What else would he want to discuss with her father?"

"I'm picturing a country wedding."

"There's only one week until he leaves. I don't think there is time for that kind of planning."

"Right on. Maybe the priest will marry them."

"Maybe so." Kay took a huge bite of the apple. "Maybe it's been planned for a while. Did you see the way she flew from here? Like all of the Royal Guard were on her heels!"

"I thought so, too. I better head home. My mum will be worried." Constance closed the door behind her, letting herself out onto the street.

Kay made dinner. She and Anthony enjoyed dining in front of the radio. They listened for updates about London and the recent blitz there. Their older brother Jimmy, who was just two years older than Kay, was an Artillery Gunner on the ground there guarding the White Cliffs of Dover. It had been nearly a month since the worst of the attacks and still there hadn't been a response- no response to George's letter informing him Mum died and no response to Kay's monthly letters updating him on her day-to-day goings on. She knew he must have more important things like survival on his mind so she kept right on writing.

Sometime after midnight Kay heard the front door latch. She got up to see who it was. George stood in the kitchen drinking a glass of water.

"Well, it's done. We'll be married on Sunday before I take leave."

"Congratulations!" Kay hugged her brother tightly. "I've always loved Theresa and now we'll be sisters."

"Yes, you will. Take care of her, Katie ."

"Most certainly. We'll take care of each other."

"Now get some rest. I saw planes on the horizon. It doesn't look like they're headed this way but they're out there."

Around four o'clock the sirens sounded once more and everyone crawled down to the cellar. Kay was so tired from her job she curled up on her mother's old bed and fell right back to sleep. The rest of the week was a blur of sewing during the day only to meet Anthony outside and continue to her second job working in Trafford Park. Her job in Trafford Park came with additional bus privileges. At the war plant Kay worked welding small bobbins for the wireless radios intended for the Spitfires. Anthony worked assembling air craft engines for the Spitfire and Lancaster Bombers. They worked unceasingly for days and by Saturday night they were both glad they'd have Sunday off.

George's wedding was to be a simple affair. An early morning gathering with a full mass being said. Only Theresa's father and Elizabeth were in attendance. It would be impossible for her entire family to return from the countryside. While it was simple and the attendants were few, it was beautiful. Theresa wore a white dress made from a muslin tablecloth she had on hand and a veil donated by Martha. George wore a neat blue shirt borrowed from a neighbour and stunning navy slacks! The wedding was completed by noon and the young couple disappeared for a short honeymoon in the countryside before he was scheduled to depart a mere six hours later.

Constance, Veronica and Kay were invited to a small wedding reception hosted by Hilda. Hilda and her husband lived in neighbouring Wigan where the effects of months of Luftwaffe hadn't been felt. Looking out the train car window Kay remembered Wigan from her childhood years where she attended St. Frances' School for Girls. Her early years in Wigan were happy ones. Her father was a paraplegic as a result of a railway accident. He worked as a train engineer for the years prior to her birth. Then, when she was very small, the fateful accident occurred. He subsequently suffered a stroke due to brain injury and his paralyses was complicated by it. Though all of Kay's memories were of him in a wheelchair, he had been a loving and active father.

They spent many days watching the trains pass behind their small home near the tracks. He taught her to set her watch by the trains. Now he was gone. He'd died so suddenly that autumn night in 1936, with little warning. They'd moved to Manchester by then. Kay recalled her mother waking her in the middle of the night asking her to go to Martha's to fetch two long white tapers for his wake. Numbly she went and did as she was asked. Martha was kind and held her while she cried. That evening marked the beginning of loss. Losses that continued with this wretched war and her mother's death.

"Kay . Are you ill?"

"No. I'm not bothered."

She knew she was fibbing but it was such a pleasant day for everyone else, she didn't want to bring them down. Going to Wigan was difficult for her. She knew her mother's only sister, Mary, would be at the reception. It wasn't that she didn't want to see her, only that her resemblance to her own recently deceased Mum was so striking. Even her mannerisms would bring back painful memories, reminding her of her mother's recent passing. The train stopped and the three girls got off. They walked the remaining distance to Hilda's home located on Hodges Street. They passed the pier, the park, and the street where her childhood home was tucked away. Kay said a silent prayer.

At Hilda's home the garden gate stood open and music drifted through the front door welcoming them. Aunt Mary rushed out to give her a squeeze.

"I'm sorry about, Bessie. We all miss her. I would've come, yet with the unusual circumstances and no wake- well I wasn't sure what to do really."

"It's all right. We're getting along well."

"Come in and have a bite to eat and a cup of tea. Hilda has really outdone herself in the kitchen."

Kay introduced Constance and Veronica. Her aunt shook their hands.

"It's quite odd having a wedding reception where the bride and groom are absent." Kay thought aloud.

"Not really. They've so little time. Wait until your wedding day. They've much more important things to attend to." Constance waggled her eyebrows. Kay smacked Constance's thigh.

"A lady shan't say such things."

"Maybe not but it is the truth and since when do I care what a lady should say?"

"Say, who is the good looking gentleman near the tea service?" Interest peeked in Veronica's eyes.

"My cousin, Edward. He isn't in the military. He has problems with his vision and they wouldn't take him."

"I'll bet he is grateful now."

"Not really. While he'll say the military didn't suit him I know it really weighs heavily on him."

"Please introduce me." Veronica grabbed Kay's hand and led the way to where Edward was standing. Kay gladly made the introductions. Within moments Veronica and Edward were lost in conversation. Constance and Kay exchanged knowing smiles and went outside to find a seat in the courtyard.

"First Theresa, now Veronica. Are we to be lonely old maids throughout this war?"

"They're not married yet. Besides I'm holding out for a G.I." Constance sipped her tea.

"A G.I.?"

"Yes. An American Soldier."

"What makes you think they're coming?"

"I heard a few older gentlemen discussing it with my father the other evening. The Americans will join us in this war. They came to our defence in the first World War- this will be no different."

"I don't know about that. They don't have a dog in this fight."

"Not yet, but they will and when they do I want to date an American G.I."

"A Yank? You want to date a bloody Yank?"

"I sure do. Tell me there's nothing more handsome than a G.I. And their accent? Have you ever heard it?"

"No."

"Well, you'll know when you do. Turn you to pudding with one word."

"Connie!"

Kay turned bright red and downed the rest of her tea in one giant gulp. She shoved a huge bite of crumpet into her mouth- covered in butter! It had been months since she had eaten anything this delectable and she savoured every last bite.

"Keep eating like that and you'll increase my chances of attracting all of their attentions."

"You can have them. I'm not interested. I've heard about them and their mistreatment of women. I for one won't be one of them! My father would roll over in his grave as soon as see me court one of them!"

"Perfect. More for me."

The remainder of the afternoon was spent discussing the war effort, the blitz, the fates of France and Poland. War seemed to occupy every thought and every aspect of life. Other than her cousin Edward and the much older married gentlemen, Constance was right- there wasn't a single other eligible male present. When a dance played, only Edward and Veronica waltzed in the garden. The older couples applauded when they finished. Constance looked at Kay and stuck out her tongue. By five o'clock, it was time to catch the train home. The railway service would stop at dusk, not wanting to risk passengers getting caught between destinations and trapped by an air raid.

On the ride home, Veronica was aglow and Constance was sulking, while Kay was emotionally worn out. Anthony rode back with them. He seemed to already be missing George having said their goodbyes this same morning after the wedding. When Anthony and Kay arrived home over an hour later they returned to an empty, lonely house. Both made their way to their bedrooms in anticipation of the bombing which would certainly come.

The next eleven months of their lives were spent working both day and night. Kay got Anthony a job repairing sewing machines during the day at Harry's shop. She liked having him with her. It was the only way she could be sure of his safety. They'd work until the end of their shift and then they'd continue to Stretford where they each worked at welding small aircraft parts as well as assembling the much larger engines. At the end of nearly a year they were both trained on every assembly line at the plant. Anthony was a quick study and became a sort of floater. He was used wherever needed to cover absences, illnesses and even injuries. The machinery they operated was dangerous, but neither of them ever gave a second thought to their own safety.

During the long second shift, which ran from six o'clock in the evening to two o'clock in the morning, air raids would often break out. The building would be under fire and everyone would crouch beneath their work stations praying to survive. The blacked out window panes would rattle and on bad nights several would shatter. The lights flickered on and off. They lost power on more than one occasion, but as soon as it passed everyone would return to work as if nothing happened. What work could be done without overhead lighting and power would get done using old fashioned lanterns. Since there weren't any buses running at this time of night, they would walk the several blocks home and begin the next day anew.

At Harry's, Kay began hand stitching her note on a bit of scrap fabric due to the severe paper shortage. She continued the process at night while sitting in front of the radio. It was time consuming, but she couldn't discontinue it. At work she would then fold the piece of fabric into the folds of each parachute. The parachutes would be inspected by the bombing squadron who would receive them before use. Each note was the same as the ones she previously placed in the trouser pockets.

Be safe. God bless. Xoxo Kay

For some of the other girls hand stitching the notes was gruelling and required precious extra seconds they didn't have. So while Hilda, Veronica and Theresa discontinued the practise, both Constance and Kay continued on. Kay had no idea what Constance's notes said and wasn't sure she wanted to. With Constance you could never be sure. Kay figured it was probably curt and humorous-maybe even a little racy. Constance once jokingly claimed it was her way to warm every G.I.'s heart.

The winter came again and the news of Pearl Harbour reached Britain. The radio in the sewing shop told of the horrible atrocities there and as the death toll rose Kay realised Constance had been correct. The Americans would join with Allied forces and hopefully this God forsaken war would come to an end. All of the girls listened attentively as the radio announcer spoke of the United States. Even Harry stopped working, called Anthony from the back room and ordered all sewing to halt. He couldn't hear the radio over the din made by the machines.

Everyone sat in stilled silence hanging onto every word. The announcement had been made. The G.I.'s were coming and Constance let out a squeal of delight!

After the broadcast ended it was back to work for the remainder of the shift. Everyone sewed with renewed zeal. By midafternoon a courier brought a communication for Harry. Harry read it and then stood behind the till, turning the radio down as he did.

"Ladies, it seems we're being called into service once again. This current shipment of parachutes is being redirected to nearby Burtonwood where the United States Army will soon arrive. The order has been upped to fifteen hundred parachutes by the end of the month. We'll need more help. If there is anyone you know of who can aid in this effort, please notify them immediately of our needs."

"My aunt is an excellent seamstress, her children are grown. I'll contact her."

"Splendid, Kay. I mean anyone- literally anyone at all who can operate a sewing machine can be trained in a matter of days."

"I can do it." Anthony stepped forward. "But if news of this sewing bit is ever spoken to my brothers or any of my other mates..."

"Wonderful, Anthony, and in the spirit of teamwork I'll add my talents as well." Harry walked over and clapped Anthony on the back.

#

Christine watched as her grandmother's face took on animated zeal. She spoke of the allied forces and their arrival at Burtonwood- as well as other bases. The news spread throughout the whole of England and with it hope. Christine thought of her own generation and their perception of war as a far away act of violence. It never really affected Americans' homes or daily lifestyles- unless you were a military family. It always amazed her the way the entire free world came together in unity to defend freedom, liberty, and life. She'd never experienced anything like it in her lifetime and hoped to never have to. She wondered if she were called to do as they had- could she do it?

Chapter Five

October 1942

D'Coteau Air Field

North Brookfield, Massachusetts

"I think she's all set. How much time until Mr. Pierre comes by to take her for a flight?"

"About an hour." Robert answered.

"That's plenty."

"You know what Pop said about flying the clients' planes, Ray."

"Yeah. But this time it's a necessary test flight. Stop

worrying old woman."

"Don't say I didn't warn you."

Ray pushed the small plane out of the hanger, donned his goggles, and climbed in. Within moments he was gone. Flying high over the North Brookfield countryside. Beyond the small farms and apple orchards. Over tree tops where clear blue sky meets with wispy white clouds. Flying brings with it peace and tranquillity- an experience like no other.

He passed a herd of dairy cattle grazing below him on the Frank Family Dairy. Looking at his watch he knew he'd better turn back now or risk discovery by Pop but just couldn't bring himself to do so. Fear of discovery and the resulting punishment were worth the few extra moments of bliss flying offered. Pop taught him everything he knew about flight and shared his passion for it, but he drew the line at flying customers' planes. Ray was a wild pilot with an adventurous spirit. He'd nearly crash landed two planes just a few years earlier when he'd taken the literal approach to coming in on a wing and a prayer- just to see if he could.

On one of those occasions he'd stayed out beyond what was sensible and to no one's surprise found himself on empty. He was miles from the nearest air strip and knew the farm fields near his house were his best bet. They were relatively even and smooth-cleared of trees or other large plants. The cows and other farm animals would mind the temporary intrusion but would be unharmed. Aside from the traumatised girl he'd had riding shotgun, no one else would be bothered or so he thought. Her father was the chief of police over in Worchester and it turns out he was bothered more than Ray expected he'd be.

In the end, Pop appeased him by agreeing to six months of community service and no charges on Ray's record- as well as a promise Ray would remain far away from his daughter. Since then Ray was careful to plan his outings when Pop was not scheduled to return to the shop for hours. Today was different. The desire to fly this exquisite plane must be his only excuse. He let temptation get the better of him.

Test flights needed to be done to check planes after they were repaired, making sure they were in working order, but after his flight record his father reduced him to mechanic work only. Of course he still flew their own family planes, but several of the clients' planes were newer, swifter models. Their sleek, manoeuverable designs made his puddle jumper seem antiquated and sluggish. Ray had wanted to fly this plane since the day it had arrived at their small airstrip a few weeks earlier. Today he saw an opportunity and he seized it. He liked to take risks and Pop didn't appreciate that. Today's test flight would be no exception.

He rounded the landing strip and radioed the tower on approach. Lou's usual voice was clipped and short. Pop must have been standing right there.

"All clear for landing, Ray."

Ray set his plane down with gentle finesse and sidled it up to the hanger where his brother and the other mechanics stood with a military man. Pop stood among them as well. Ray opened the hatch and climbed down.

Pop walked over to him and introduced the gentleman as Paul.

"Paul is here from Ft. Devens. He's come in search of pilots and aeroplane mechanics."

Pop seemed worried and tense. His shoulders pushed back tightly, the line of his mouth grim where his pipe peaked out from the corner.

"Nice to meet you, Paul. Are you a military recruiter?"

"I am. Specifically for mechanics and pilots. This mess overseas is going to require a lot of mechanics and pilots and I don't have the time necessary to train a bunch of newbies. I've got an abbreviated course for experienced airmen and mechanics."

"How long are we talking?"

"Twelve weeks of specialized training plus basic training. Then straight over to England to Base Air Depot 1 Burtonwood, a place we call BAD1."

"How long overseas?"

"Could be anywhere from a year to years. No one knows for sure with a campaign this size."

"I'll bet we kick their Nazi asses in less than six months." Francis boasted from behind Ray where he was working on the grinder.

"Don't be so sure." Pop warned.

Paul walked over to where Robert and Ray stood at the entrance of the hanger.

"I don't need a decision today but please consider it. You'll be doing an amazing service to your country. The US Army would be happy to have your assistance."

Paul turned to address the rest of the mechanic shop.

"The offer extends to all of you, aged eighteen or older. I'm in need of pilots and aeroplane mechanics."

He set a stack of business cards down on the desk at the door and shook Pop's hand thanking him.

As soon as he was out of sight, Pop made an announcement.

"Get back to work. I'm not paying you to stand around and catch flies. Ray and Robert- in my office."

"Here comes the whipping for the test flight. Thanks for dragging me into this Ray."

Ray and Robert walked sluggishly into their father's office.

"Take a seat boys."

When both had done as they were asked he lit a match and took several short puffs to get his pipe lit.

"This war is nasty business boys. Not to be taken lightly. You're both too young to know much about World War I but I remember. A lot of life lost over there. A lot left and never came home. However as mechanics you'd be on the ground, and except for air raids, you should be out of harm's way. As pilots, it would be another story with lots of risk involved. ”

"So, you think we should go."

"I think going would be the honourable thing to do but not without risk. Don't think I didn't notice the little stunt you pulled today. This stint in the military may be just what the two of you need. Some discipline."

"Will you be all right without us, Pop?" Robert asked.

"I'll have Francis. Your cousin's not old enough to enlist. I think with the war things will be fairly slow here. All of the steel is going to the war effort. Parts will be difficult to get. I served as did your grandfather before me. It's your turn."

"Then, it's settled." Ray stood taking his hat in his hand. He clapped his father's back as he hugged him. Robert did the same.

The men walked out of the office and to the hanger where they began working on an engine.

"What do you think?"

"I don't know. It sounds like Pop wants us to go- as mechanics. He doesn't sound as excited about the prospect of us being pilots. I've gotta be honest here Ray- I'm not excited about that part either. Flying over there is dangerous. I heard this broadcast on the radio about the air raids in London. It's a nasty piece of work this war business. I love flying planes but I've got no desire to die in one."

Robert was three years older than Ray. He'd always possessed a calm demeanour and a timidity Ray lacked. His cautious reluctance kept him out of trouble and Ray knew he should listen to him on this account where he'd failed to do so many times before.

"I think it sounds like fun! Whooping up on those nitwit Germans. The whole thing will be over and done with in a few months time." Francis spoke like the sixteen year old kid he was.

"I don't think so, Francis." Then, Robert turned his gaze on Ray. "Promise me you're not going to sign on as a pilot. I've heard other vets talk about conflicts. Flying missions and bombing targets. There can be huge civilian casualties- huge losses. You know Earl from the gas station. His daughter told me he still has nightmares about World War I. At least as mechanics we'll be somewhat removed from the battle. Just give it some thought. Don't let your love of flying be forever diminished by war."

"I can't say I don't agree with you- I do. I have no desire to go running off to war and get myself killed. Besides- who'll dance with Dorothy if I'm dead?"

"Dorothy, Margaret, Nancy- I guess they'd be forced to go out and find an honourable man who wants to do more than dance with them and lift their skirts every Saturday night."

"Isn't that what I'm supposed to be doing? It's better than your near priest-like existence. You're the oldest son of a French Canadian family- not of an Irish family."

"I'm glad he's going off- maybe Nancy will take a liking to me while he's gone." Francis joked from where he was watching this charade, smoking a cigarette.

"Put that out. Too young to smoke, too young for Nancy too." Ray chimed.

"I've got a plan. If we go off and do this thing I'm going to come right back here. Run things for Pop and marry Betsy." Robert announced.

"Betsy Long? You haven't even gone on a date with her yet! You'd better get started if you're talking marriage."

"Shows what you know. I went out with her last weekend. Ma and Pop love her. I ate dinner with her folks this week. Things are progressing nicely."

"Kind of jumping into this whole marriage bit don't you think?"

"You know when it's right. Besides I'm planning on after the war. She'll wait for me. You'll see."

"I'll just sit back and watch- take notes. Learn from your mistakes."

Robert reached over and pelted his brother on the shoulder. Next he grabbed him around the neck in a choke hold and a wrestling match ensued. Pop came out a few moments later and broke it up. They finished up for the day and headed for home. On their way home, Ray rode in silence in the backseat of the car. He pulled the business card out of his jacket pocket and looked it over carefully.

"You're going to do it?" Robert asked.

"Not a doubt in my mind."

"Okay- then we'll do it together. What does the card say?"

"There's a recruiting office over in Boston. He wrote tomorrow's date on the back, *10 o'clock. See you there.*"

Pop simply nodded his head from where he sat behind the steering wheel smoking his pipe between clinched teeth.

"You boys be smart about this and be careful. You must tell your mother."

Pop parked their car inside the barn. They walked up the short walkway to the house. Inside Ma set dinner on the table. The savoury smell of meatloaf, mashed potatoes, gravy, and glazed carrots greeted them. They both disappeared down the hall to wash the black grease from their hands. She had a very strict *no washing filthy hands in my kitchen sink* policy. Robert and Ray agreed in the bathroom that Robert, as the older brother, should be the one to tell their mother.

At the table a short time later she surprised them by asking

"So - did Paul come find you down at the hanger?"

"He did. You knew?"

"Well he stopped by here first. While I don't like the idea of you boys going off to war- we live in a free country. Defending freedom and liberty is what we do. If I were younger I'd have half a mind to enlist myself. I'm not a nurse or anything but I know how to bandage a wound."

"Then, it's settled. There's a meeting tomorrow in Boston."

"He said as much." Their father spoke between bites of

meatloaf.

"I'm proud of my boys. You can go. You have my blessing but you have to write to me- and write often. No fooling around with the girls overseas. I don't want my first grandchild to be born in a foreign country during a war!" With these words Ma made the sign of the cross.

"Ma, Pop- I plan on asking Betsy to marry me before I go."

"Perfect, son. I'd say you were crazy but there's something about the two of you. You'll make it. I'm sure of it." Pop commented. "What about you son? You going to break things off with the half dozen or so you've been seeing?"

"Maybe so."

Less than two weeks later they started Basic Training at Ft. Devens, Massachusetts. Basic Training was followed by a 12 week crash course at an aeroplane engine mechanic school in Dearborn, Michigan for Robert. Ray's flight school training was just as swift and intense. Then, just as Paul explained, they were deployed to Burtonwood as part of the Army Air Force with Headquarters Squadron 51st Troop Carrier Wing in the Mighty Eight Air Force. The base was enormous with men in the thousands stationed there. It was the single largest Royal Air Force base in Europe. The hangers were endless and while B-17's were the primary planes, there were countless others. Robert's main task was the overhauling of aircraft engines. There was no shortage of work. Ray was to co-pilot a B-17 Flying Fortress on missions over the channel.

In a matter of a few weeks Robert was deployed to Rattlesden Airfield in Suffolk over two hundred miles away, while Ray stayed behind at BAD1. Rattlesden was a much smaller camp and Ray knew even though it was smaller it would be no less of a military target. Ray and Robert prayed for each other's safety and promised to write.

Ray's routine was the same day after day. Up at four thirty for breakfast. Meeting at five thirty. Workday commences at five forty-five. Long shifts and very little sleep. Pilots and mechanics from all over the United States were recruited. Some mechanics were aeroplane mechanics who'd already known plane engines, but most were auto mechanics. Ray flew with some amazing men. The B-17 crews consisted of ten members: two co-pilots, a navigator, a flight engineer/top-turret gunner, five additional gunners, and a radio operator. The constant roar of plane engines could be heard both inside and out. Missions were scheduled and then needed to be scrubbed frequently due to low visibility and poor weather. The Cheshire weather proved to be wet and dreary, as was the case over most of England.

On their days off, Ray and his friends ventured into neighbouring Warrington. On one Sunday he and the other crew members were given new uniform slacks to wear when not working. Their others were well worn. The new ones were a welcome sight. Each went through the stack selecting his size.

Ray seized a pair and immediately put them on. He felt something in the pocket and pulled it out. Each man did the same. They all held up small folded notes procured from their trousers' pockets.

"What's yours say?" Ray directed his question to Dick from Detroit who was fast becoming a good friend.

"Come find me and say hello. Constance "

All the men whistled at the invitation.

"I don't know that I can top that. Mine says Be safe. God bless. Xoxo Kay "

"I wonder where these slacks were made."

Dick searched the waistband finding a tag. It read *Harry's. Manchester, Lancs.*

"Well, it looks like you have your answer."

"Why not take a trip into Manchester today? Track these gals down and thank them properly for the slacks. I think they'll want to see how nicely they fit." Dick teased.

"I don't know if I want to track this one down." Pete read the small note which fell out of his slacks.

"What's it say?"

"Kill the bastards. Hilda."

All of the men laughed at his note.

"She sounds angry- that one!"

"She sounds scary as heck! Even her name- Hilda. She doesn't sound British at all. You get Constance and Kay - I have Hilda."

"Could be worse. You could have no trousers at all. Besides-Dick wants to track down Constance and we've got nothing better to do today."

It was settled. Their weekly trip into Warrington was tossed out the proverbial window and replaced by a journey to Manchester some twenty plus miles away. They caught a ride with another group travelling in that direction. A short while later they were dropped off on the outskirts of town. After walking into Manchester and asking directions from a salesclerk in a corner store, it didn't take them long to locate Harry's- but being it was Sunday the shop was closed. The front door locked.

"Bright idea, Detroit Dick." Ronald chided.

"We'll have to come back, is all."

"Come on. We might as well see the sights while we're here." Ray led the way through the streets of Manchester until he located a bar at the Plymouth Grove Hotel.

"It says here they have Bass in the bottle. Sounds like my kind of place."

"On Sunday?" Ray questioned. No one else seemed to care so he followed them inside.

The five men made their way across the room and took a seat at the bar. There was a group of beautiful young girls sitting at a table snacking on fish and chips. Detroit Dick decided he'd walk over to introduce himself. The others sipped their beers betting he'd get shot down in less than sixty seconds.

From the bar they could see Dick talking with a beautiful brunette. She invited him to pull up a chair to sit with the three of them.

"Can you believe he's gone and done it?" Ronald sounded impressed.

The other four walked over and dragged a table and pub stools over to join him on his mission.

"Let me introduce the ladies. This is Constance, Agnes, and Susan. Constance and I were just discussing how I'm wearing her slacks. I took her up on her invitation to 'Come say hello'."

"And I'm so glad he did." Constance drank her pint.

"Awe- so these are the gals who work at Harry's?"

"No, just Constance. Agnes and Susan work in the war plant across town."

Ray pulled the note from Kay out of his pocket and handed it to Constance .

"Would you happen to know this lady?"

"I would but I'll make no promise to introduce you. She doesn't date G.I.'s. Her five brothers have strictly forbidden it."

"Five brothers? I'll bet. That's surely a shame. I had no

intention of a date but to thank her rather."

Agnes and Susan looked at each other.

"Then, you haven't seen Kay." Susan laughed.

"So that's why she requires the protection of five brothers? She's that beautiful? Now I have to meet her."

"She's a real looker. All the blokes around here like her as well but she won't give them any consideration." Susan interjected.

"She uptight?" Ronald asked.

"No, both her parents have died- her mum recently. She takes care of her youngest brother, as well as working in the war effort."

"Are all of her older brothers away?"

"They're all serving. Stationed everywhere from here to Scotland."

"So none are at home with her- other than the youngest."

"Making sure you're not going to get pounded wicked bad when you look her up- are you Ray?" Ronald engaged.

All the men laughed.

"I'm just trying to figure her story out is all. So we've got a young, beautiful lady living on her own raising a younger brother. Working a job."

"Two jobs actually."

"Well, no wonder she doesn't get out- she's exhausted. Gentleman- I think this girl is in need of our help. Where does she live? It's a Sunday. Certainly she's not working today."

"Oh no. If you want to meet her you'll have to track her down on your own." Constance accepted a lit cigarette from Dick.

"Look- even the girls are frightened of her!" Dick howled. "I think their pulling your leg. She's probably over seven feet tall, built like a lineman and a terrible witch."

"Not Kay, she's nice- if you're going to be frightened by a woman on our sewing crew it would be Hilda. She'll eat you up and spit you out."

"I told you so!" Pete exploded in laughter, the other men joining in. Ray was quick to explain.

"Pete here received a rather colourful, explicit directive from Hilda in his slacks. He was actually afraid to look her up."

"That's good because she is already married."

Pete seemed to breath a sigh of relief hearing Hilda was off the market and his friends wouldn't expect him to ask her out. Susan changed the subject. She wanted to know more about the Army Air

Force. This was her first opportunity to question a group of American GI's and she took it. The group sat and visited until it was time for the men to return to Burtonwood. The girls walked them to the station and waved goodbye from the platform.

Ray wasn't sure why but he couldn't get this Kay girl out of his head. She sounded like a strange mixture of sweet and pretty mixed with a little tough as nails. Any girl who lived on her own, worked two jobs and brought up a little brother- all in wartime England- must be strong. The more he thought about it, the more determined he became to meet this woman. Of course he could be hugely disappointed. Maybe the girls were teasing him- but there was something about her note.

Be safe. God bless. XOXO Kay

The simple, kind tone to it coupled with the blessing. This girl had to be something special!

#

"So Grandpa thought you were a dog?" Christine interjected intrigued by her grandmother's account of Ray and his friends' visit to Manchester.

"At least he thought it was a possibility."

"So he went in search of you?"

"Not yet. A lot more happened before I ever met him."

"Get to the good stuff Grandma. Details- I want details."

Chapter Six

November 1942

The G.I.'s continued to come and wartime England changed

instantly. They were everywhere at once...in the shops, on the trains

and in the pubs. Kay went about her daily routine- work, work and

more work. Constance had gone G.I. *crazy!* From dances to parties,

she and several of their other friends could be seen on the arm of a

different G.I. every Friday or Saturday night.

Kay was more afraid of them than anything else. She'd heard

the girls talking about how British girls could easily get into trouble

with these men. To them women were expendable and they were

looking for no more than a good time while the war lasted. Some of them even had steady girlfriends back home! Kay decided the best way to steer clear of the entire mess was to avoid it altogether!

One day when she arrived home from work she and Anthony were greeted by the letter carrier. He held a box of letters for them. They eagerly raced inside. Among them she found letters from her four brothers- all alive and well. They were tired and ready to come home but still dedicated to the war effort. As she opened one letter after another, sharing each with Anthony, it was Anthony who spied some official looking envelopes in the box.

"What are these?"

Knowing her brothers were all safe and sound, Kay was certain they couldn't be notifications of the bad sort.

"Open them and see."

"They're addressed to you."

"Go on. Open them."

Anthony opened the first one and his eyes widened.

"Katie, it's money."

"Money? What sort?"

Anthony thrust the paper at her.

"As in the cheque sort and it is quite a lot."

"Open the other ones then."

Kay picked the cheque up off the table and examined it closely. Anthony was right. It was money and lots of it. All these months she'd waited for her brothers' war benefit cheques and here they were.

"How many are there in all?'

"It appears there are ten, so far. They are all dated from a while back. It means there are more coming- right?"

"Apparently so. I'm not certain, but I'd assume so. What shall we do with them?"

"Well, I think the right thing to do would be to set the money aside in an account for each of them for after the war. It is their money after all and most of the things I'd like to buy aren't available for any amount anyhow."

"How mature you've become, Anthony. Yes- you're right. I think we should only touch the money if we need it. We've been doing fairly well for ourselves without it, haven't we?"

"Aye, we have."

"There is one thing though. I have been giving thought to

turning our house into a sort of halfway house."

"A halfway house?"

"Yes, for non-military men and women helping in the war effort. There have been many who have come and are working in the factories alongside us. If we open our home to them at no charge, maybe others will come as well. We have enough machines at Harry's to run three shifts- we only lack the people."

"Perhaps if we reach out to those in the countryside there will be others who will help and with only a little from these cheques we'd have enough to cover our expenses."

"What a wonderful idea- now to convince Harry."

"I don't think it'll take much convincing. When you're doing things with a good heart and for the right reasons things have a way of working themselves out."

Kay was awed at her little brother's integrity and commitment. He was still very young but this war was making him a man. Each day he was changing right before her eyes. No longer the thin boy of childhood, his shoulders were broadening and his jaw becoming more defined. His baby fat was gone and had been replaced by muscle from their work in the factory. She wished her parents were here to see him and how he'd grown.

The following day a short conversation with Harry proved Kay to be correct. He thought the idea magnificent and agreed to employ any able seamstresses who came his way. A trip to the local newspaper and it was settled. Within a few weeks of starting the ad there were three shifts of women working tirelessly. To Kay's surprise many of them loved the idea of placing personalised notes with each parachute.

Both Kay and Anthony made the difficult decision to cut their hours at the war plant back to only two nights each week. Their house was filled to overflowing but with it came a band of characters so lively and entertaining that neither of them seemed to mind the crowded conditions. Mostly women came- women from all over. Some came and went while others stayed for months at a time. Young women with brothers fighting in the war, older women with sons and husbands. The three bedrooms and cellar housed small cots wall-to-wall. Through combining rations there was always enough to go around. The women always cooked for each other making sure to each do her share. For Kay, life returned to her small row house and with it came happiness.

There was one mother-daughter team who arrived from Morecambe. They were the only two remaining at home and found themselves feeling useless. Bette, the mother, and Edith, her daughter, had four men serving England. Her husband, Herbert, and their three sons- Edmund, Liam, and Oliver- had all gone off to war. When they saw the advertisement in the paper, they packed their bags and came. They even refused payment from Harry, insisting this was the least they could do. They committed to staying until the end of the war and for this reason Kay gave them her parents' room upstairs.

Edith was a black haired beauty of fifteen, the same age as Anthony, and Kay knew it hadn't escaped Anthony's notice. Upon their arrival he asked Kay to cut his hair- it was his first haircut in months! He shined his shoes and even pressed his own trousers and shirts. He switched his sewing shift to third shift, working from two o'clock in the morning until eight o'clock insisting the ladies on the night shift required a male escort home- for safety reasons of course. Edith gladly accepted his chivalrous offer and each night came home on his arm.

Now seventeen and rapidly approaching eighteen, Kay's life

was so filled to capacity she possessed time for little else.

"Come dancing with us tonight."

Constance's voice behind her at her machine startled her.

"Why would I?"

"You know why. Besides Veronica, Theresa, and I think you are in very serious danger of becoming a spinster."

"I don't know. A dance might be nice. Can you promise me there won't be any of your infamous G.I.'s there?"

"What kind of silly nonsense is that? Of course there will be G.I.'s there. Loads of them! Bushels of them! What? Are you afraid you might actually have a good time?"

"Of course not. I like to have a good time."

"But you feel guilty about it is all. I know how you must feel." Constance sat on the edge of her sewing table. "All of your brothers off at war. Cold, dirty and miserable. Do you think it would make them happy to know you're making yourself miserable as well?"

"No. I'm not miserable exactly, just not pursuing fun filled activities."

"You are miserable. Look at you. You're sitting on

mountains of hard earned money, you're a seamstress, and your clothes are so thread bare you look like a pauper."

Kay looked at her dress. She had worn it until it was worn out and thread bare. Constance was right.

"What should I do?"

"Come with us tonight. There is a USO dance. It promises to be filled with dancing, spirits and fun. I'll bring you a frock after work and please wash your hair."

Kay stood staring at herself in the bathroom mirror at home some time later. She had to acknowledge the accuracy of Constance's assessment of her. She used to take such pride in her appearance back before the war began. Her mother would painstakingly pin curl her hair every night so the curls cascaded in ringlets down her back, across her brow and around her face. Today her hair hung in two loose braids- remnants left from last night. She'd not even taken the time to comb or brush her hair since the day before.

Her eyes looked tired and her colour was ashen. Then there was her dress. She should have been embarrassed to be seen outside her home in such untidy clothing. Kay herself was a seamstress! She could locate enough fabric around the house to fashion a few new dresses- maybe even a suit complete with a blouse or two. Bolts of fabric sat stacked in her bedroom cupboard. She didn't know why she refused to do for herself anymore. She was ashamed of herself. Her mother never would've approved of her current state.

Today the mourning comes to an end. Today life begins anew. Serving my country and honouring my brothers in no way means I must become a slovenly hermit.

Kay scrubbed her hair and rolled it in rollers while it was still damp. She went to her cupboard where she'd placed a small box filled with her mother's toiletries. In it she found perfume and lipstick which would have to double as rouge. Kay was blessed with a clear complexion and ivory skin. It didn't take much and she looked like a doll. She heard the front door and Constance came skipping up the stairs.

"Much better. I thought I'd have to tie you and scrub you myself."

Constance carried two frocks. One was a bright red dress with a fitted jacket, the other one was a long fitted purple skirt with a kick pleat in the back, a cream coloured blouse and a short fitted jacket with cuffed sleeves.

"I think the red one will look best with your complexion and lipstick, but I know you're a fan of purple so I brought both. Keep them. They're gifts."

"Thank you. In honour of the British Jack I'll wear the red one. I like the ruffle flared hemline. You don't think the top will be a little too snug for me?"

"Try it on. Let's see."

Kay carefully shimmied it down over her hair, still in rollers- then slid it down over her shoulders and hips. It fit like a glove.

"Perfect."

Kay gave herself the once over in the mirror and had to admit she looked great. Even between the large cracks in the mirror she could see her entire length when she stepped back and stood on tiptoe.

"Now for earrings and a dab of perfume to complete the ensemble."

"And silk stockings." Constance stood holding a black marking pencil.

"Silk stockings? Where are we going to find those? Even

with all the money in the world there are none to be had."

"Maybe not. That is why we're making them. Now turn around."

Constance used the pencil to trace a line all the way down the back of Kay's upper thigh and calf to her black leather heals.

"You are crafty, Constance ."

"I think so and in the dim lights of the dance hall no one will be able to tell they're not stockings. You'll be the envy of every girl there. How long before your hair dries?"

"Another ten minutes."

"Perfect. Agnes and Susan are meeting us outside the hall in half an hour."

Kay had known both Agnes and Susan since moving to Manchester. They were among the worldlier of Constance's friends. Susan was known mostly for really enjoying herself and on many occasions overdoing it a little. The last Kay heard she'd been dating a mate of theirs quite seriously before the war. It was rumoured they may even have gotten married. Kay dismissed this rumour, as she did most rumours, since she couldn't imagine Susan was married in light of the fact she was out going to parties most weekends with other men.

Agnes didn't have a serious boyfriend. Kay's brothers said while she regularly enjoyed a pint or two, all in all she was a good girl. While they both were always more than nice to Kay, and she was sure they would continue being gracious towards her, spending an entire evening in their company wasn't all too appealing. Everything considered though, they were merely going dancing. Kay decided not to bother herself too much about it and hoped for the best. She ripped the curlers out of her hair and fluffed it prettily. She stepped carefully downstairs to meet Constance and they were off at a brisk pace to meet the others.

Outside the hall there were two men smoking cigarettes. When one's intense gaze met her own, Kay instinctively looked away. She sensed he found her attractive and while the feeling was mutual, she was here to dance- maybe laugh a little and share a drink. Getting involved with a GI, no matter where he was from, was an entirely different matter altogether. From the look he was giving her he seemed interested in a lot more than casual conversation and dancing. She decided to avoid his stare completely and breeze past him without a backwards glance.

Inside the hall they could barely see Agnes and Susan for the flock of G.I.'s surrounding them. Constance had been right- most of them were attractive and very nicely turned out. At Constance and Kay's approach many of them hooted and hollered. They were quite the rowdy bunch.

Suddenly the gentleman from outside was there front and centre. Kay wondered how he'd made it inside the hall and to the table ahead of her. He was quick.

"Constance, who's your friend?" He asked, cigarette poised on the edge of his lower lip.

"This is Kay ."

Kay was immediately flanked by a good looking G.I. on either side offering to escort her onto the dance floor. She felt intimidated, unused to all this male attention, especially from G.I.'s. Then the gentleman with the cigarette stepped forward to take her hand, handing his cigarette to the G.I. on her right side. He was quite handsome with warm hazel eyes and a devilish grin. A lock of hair escaped his uniform hat and fell over his forehead in a sexy curl.

"Thank you for coming to meet me, Kay, would you like to dance?"

He kissed her hand and then neatly tucked it around his arm.

"Thank you sir for coming to my aid." Kay said in a hushed whisper so the others couldn't hear.

"Just call me Ray. And I think I'll call you Charlie."

"Are you daft or just hard of hearing Ray? My name is Kay, but you can call me Katie if you'd like." Kay yanked her arm back as they crossed the room making their way to the dance floor.

"I heard you- I just think Charlie suits you better and that's what I intend to call you."

Kay couldn't believe the arrogance of this particular GI. Were they all this pig headed? Sure he was good looking- and boy did he know it! She decided in that instant dancing with him was the last thing she was interested in. Kay turned and stormed away, leaving him standing on the dance floor- the music playing. His friends were shouting to him from across the room. Kay ignored their taunts and walked over to find Constance and the girls standing at a table in the corner.

While her back was to the dance floor she could feel him coming for her from across the room.

"Is this all the thanks I get for coming to your rescue?"

"A pack of wolves would be safer than spending another minute in your company." She spoke over her shoulder making no effort to turn around. The other girls knew better than to laugh. Kay plucked a peanut from the bowl and popped it in her mouth.

"That's Ray. What a rounder he is." Agnes sipped her pint and cut her eyes at him where he'd stopped just behind Kay's turned back.

"I wouldn't mind making a round or two with him." Susan admitted.

"Well you can have him. He is a scoundrel. I can see it in the way he moves, the way he looks, even the way he smells. He's just the type of man my brothers warned me against."

"I thought he smelled nice." Susan smiled sweetly winking at Ray. A few seconds later he must have walked away because Susan was waving to him as he went.

"There he goes, Kay. Way to run off the best looking pilot in the room."

Kay merely ignored Susan's comment. It wasn't worthy of a response. The room was milling with girls who Kay recognised and had known for years. She occasionally bumped into some of them on the bus or streetcars, but most of them she hadn't seen in months. That was confirmation enough that her life needed to revolve around something more than church and work- and the war, but she wasn't quite convinced this was it.

"Here he comes again, Kay. He can be quite persistent." Constance warned.

"I can handle him. I don't have four older brothers for nothing." But to everyone's surprise he went over to the neighbouring table and asked Julie to dance instead. He twirled Julie round and round the dance floor. After Julie it was Shirley, then Sandra and Ines. Next he worked the other side of the room where he asked Olga and Yvonne to dance.

"Well, he sure thinks he's something." Kay chided.

"And most women think so, too." Agnes added.

"Well, not this one. I'm going to the powder room. Anyone care to join me?"

All three girls shook their heads. Kay worked her way through the crowded hall and fought her way into the bathroom and up to the mirror. She took an exceptionally long time in the bathroom fiddling with her hair and twirling her dress. She wasn't sure she would emerge even if an air raid were sounded. Eventually it thinned out and she was the only person who remained. She wondered if she snuck out now whether she could escape unnoticed.

Coming to the dance had been a bad idea. A very bad idea.

Twenty minutes later she opened the door to see Ray waiting for her outside the hallway, his hands pushed into his front pockets.

"I thought you'd died in there."

"No, wishful thinking on your part. Since when is it polite to follow a lady to the loo?"

"You should be thanking me. If it weren't for me standing out here running all of the others off you'd have been met with cheers when you came out."

"Thanks, I guess."

"I haven't seen you around here. Where have you been hiding?"

"Work. I work a lot."

"What kind of work do you do?"

"Sewing mostly and assembly at the war plant."

"You don't say? What kind of assembly?"

"Anything really- even welding."

"A woman who can wield a torch. You scare me, Kay . You're dangerous."

"I'd have to say I've heard the same about you."

"That I have a torch or that I'm dangerous?" When she didn't answer he merely continued. "I do carry a torch but only for you."

"Do all the other girls buy your lines?"

"It's not a line. I asked Constance to bring you here tonight. I'm a pilot and my crew and I came in search of the girl who sewed this."

He fished into his pocket and withdrew a scrap of paper and a small piece of cloth. Kay recognised both the writing and stitchwork as her own. The inscriptions on each still clear...*Be safe. God bless. Xoxo Kay.*

"The paper came to me in a pair of trousers provided by the Royal Guard months ago. Then the note came to me in a parachute I inspected for my crew. Several of us received one. Those of us who've received your blessing have successfully flown missions without casualties. Some of us came to personally thank you. I'd like to do so properly if you'd dance with me."

Reluctantly Kay took his arm, and let him lead her to the

dance floor. She battled conflicting emotions about this particular man. One moment he was arrogant and prideful, in the next the perfect gentleman. She didn't have long to contemplate the two distinct sides of his personality before another G.I. cut-in on their dance. Then one after another the men from his crew thanked her as well. By the time the last song played Kay's feet throbbed and her legs ached. She and Constance said their goodbyes and began their walk home. A short distance from the hall they heard the cat calls of some rowdy G.I.'s behind them. They turned to see it was Ray and his friends.

Kay recognised all of them from the dance. The tallest one's name was Richard, Dick for short. His name was the simplest and easiest to remember. The two medium height ones were called Piggy Porter and Ronald Night. The first, Piggy Porter, received his name innocently enough. It turns out he had an enormous appetite which was quite shocking considering his thin frame. The second, Ronald Night, was known for his successful missions flown late at night. There was an incredibly short and stocky mate they referred to as Pee-Pee Partin. No one took the time to explain his nickname to Kay and she was relieved not to know the specifics with that one.

"See that girl right there gentleman, the one with the long legs and flowing blonde hair- I'm going to marry that girl!" Ray's slurred speech could be heard among a myriad of cheers.

"You're a bunch of crazy Yanks!" Kay yelled back over her shoulder.

"Say what you will." Ray and his friends caught up to them. "But I'm going to marry you so save all your dances for me. I'll be back in town in a month and I'll come find you."

"Go home and sleep it off."

"I'm walking you home first. All the way to your door. You have a military escort."

"Splendid."

"I think it is." Constance smiled at Ray's friend Dick.

"This better not have been a blind date." Kay cut her eyes at her.

"Whatever gives you that idea?"

"They're still back there?"

"They're still back there."

"Tell me you've met them before tonight. Or are we being followed by Jack the Ripper and his band of murderers?"

"I didn't know Jack the Ripper had a band of murderers."

"He didn't, I'm being facetious."

"Yes, I've met them before, previously at the hotel a month ago. We shared a few drinks."

"So, I can count on seeing the lot of them again."

"I'm afraid so."

Ray sprinted up beside her and started walking backwards in front of them.

"So Charlie, what are your plans four weeks from tonight?"

"I was thinking about hopping the ferry in Wigan and heading across to Ireland."

"There's no ferry running now. They stopped it months ago." Constance advised.

"Thank you, Constance."

"Oh, I see how you're gonna be. Well don't see me again if you don't want to. I'm certainly not going to beg you." Ray offered.

"Found one who wants nothing to do with you- did you Wood Chopper?" Piggy called from somewhere behind the girls.

"I guess I have. There's a first time for everything isn't there boys?"

"You sure are a cocky, conceited one. Are all American men this self-assured?"

"I'm afraid so. It's Gene Autry and all that."

"With your dancing display I was thinking more along the lines of Gene Kelly."

"I'll take it as a compliment."

Kay and Constance stopped at her door. Constance thanked the men for walking them home. It was then Kay noticed both Susan and Agnes appeared somewhere along the way and were walking arm-in-arm with Ronald Night and Pee-Pee Partin, the latter who in spite of his odd nickname was a rather charming and handsome man.

"See you around, Charlie." Ray whirled around and sprinted back to his friends. "Come on Dick. We're going to Mulvaney's Pub. Don't lag behind."

"I'll be along later. I'm going to walk Constance home."

"Night, Kay."

"Night."

Kay closed her door where she saw Edith and Anthony waiting up for her.

"Just making sure you made it home safely, Katie."

"Well, I did and now I'm going straight up to bed. Good night."

Kay wasn't quite sure how she felt about her evening out with friends. It wasn't as fun filled as she expected it to be. The various soldiers were nice enough, all with the exception of Ray. He irked her and got under her skin. If only he weren't so darned handsome.

Chapter Seven

"So, let me see if I've got this straight. When you met Grandpa you didn't even like him?"

"No. I thought he was crass and arrogant- but very good looking."

Christine laughed out loud at her grandmother's revelation. When she'd met Jeff she'd instantly liked him. He'd been a few years older than her- she recognised this part right away. He was mature and good natured, exceptionally funny and one of the hottest guys she'd ever met. She couldn't imagine falling in love with a man who she initially thought conceited and arrogant- or even the least bit crass! Her grandfather must have done something right- why else would Grandma have married him?

The flight attendant announced they'd be landing shortly. Her grandmother excused herself to use the restroom. Where had all the time gone? Ten hours passed and Christine was no closer to knowing the secrets of her grandmother's romance than she'd been before the flight. She wanted to sit and hear the rest but knew she'd have to be patient. They were just beginning their two week holiday. There would be visits with relatives and sightseeing galore to fill the days ahead.

Her grandmother returned from the restroom. As soon as she buckled her seatbelt, the plane began to be tossed about like a small twin engine rather than the large jet is was. Christine knew as the turbulence entered into its five minute mark she was turning a pale hue of green.

"It's always like this coming in before dawn over the Irish Sea. This time is a bit rougher than the last- we're coming down through the clouds now. It will smooth out shortly."

"I hope so. If it's like this going back I may have to take a ship home."

"Been there, done that. Two weeks on the Atlantic isn't much easier. Especially going into the winter months. It's not so bad. Just take a deep breath. You'll be fine."

Christine worked to focus on the landing and the fun they'd soon be having. Minutes later she felt the plane touch down. When the unfasten seatbelt sign was lit, she sluggishly stood and stretched. Her mother had slept right through it all, only roused by the movements of the other passengers within the cabin and the opening of the overhead compartments. Connie jumped up invigorated from her ten hour snooze ready to take on all of England while Christine felt horrid.

"I think we'll need a nap." Christine announced looking at Grandma who stood reluctantly rubbing her right knee.

"Agreed. I think my arthritis is acting up a bit from sitting for so long. That's the secret when you get to my age- don't stop moving. If you do you'll just sort of freeze up! It can be hard to get going again." Grandma put on her jacket and tied her own gold scarf loosely around her neck.

They slowly made their way to the baggage claim and waited on their luggage. The carrousel was full of suitcases of all different shapes and colours. Grandma's purple hardback suitcase was easy to spot. It matched the smaller case containing toiletries. Christine worked to grab them as they came around on the conveyor belt. Her own hot pink suitcase was medium sized and had wheels. She spied it on its first pass but couldn't get to it as there was a large group of tourists from New York standing between her and the carousel. Thankfully she was able to grab it on her second attempt.

Lastly they waited on her mother's luggage. The leopard print set of three large suitcases would be easy to spot among the other less vibrant and colorful luggage. After ten minutes they finally emerged. Christine worked to gather all the cases together and looked like a pack mule as she hauled them over and assisted her mother in stacking them on a luggage trolley. They walked towards the pick-up area located just outside baggage claim.

At the curb a very small car was waiting for them. A man in his early forties stood smiling warmly. Connie and Kay went over to hug him. They introduced him as Edward, her grandmother's second cousin. Christine wasn't sure what this meant exactly. Something about his mother being her grandmother's first cousin. That would make him her grandmother's second cousin, her mother's third cousin and her fourth cousin. No- that couldn't be right. She would have to figure it all out later. Right now the fatigue of the journey and a sleepless night were clouding any attempts she made at clear thought.

Edward was very helpful and worked to lift her suitcases along with the others into the back of the small compact car. Christine had visions of herself riding in the crammed backseat buried alive by luggage, but by some miracle he managed to shove it all in. They were somewhere on the outskirts of Manchester. In the car, her mother and grandmother discussed how much it all had changed since their last visits. Christine listened to the chatter trying to discern their itinerary.

From what Christine gathered they would be staying in Wigan first. She knew from her grandmother's story it was the home of her aunt during the war. In her mind Christine envisioned it being some great distance away. Her grandmother told her tales over the years about her outings in Wigan, and Christine likened the two towns and the distance between them to the distance between Tampa and Orlando. She was surprised to learn it was actually quite close to Manchester. Maybe only twenty miles or so.

Her grandmother had never learned to drive. She'd depended

on walking to get her everywhere she needed to go. It would certainly hinder a person's ability to navigate from place to place in a timely fashion. Occassionally she even took the buses. During Kay's youth in wartime England, Christine knew she'd done the same. She made use of the additional luxury of a good train system. To Christine the thought of walking most places seemed exhausting. A distance of anything more than five miles would prove a daunting task. No wonder Grandma recalled the distance between the two cities as being greater than it actually was. On foot it would have taken a long time to make the journey. She must have travelled to Wigan by train. Once you added in stops and the time to start back up again- even by train it probably required a significant amount of time.

They drove into Wigan and slowly continued through its centre. Wigan was a quaint little town filled with row houses, parks, a pier and shops. There were pubs and restaurants, as well as quite a developed shopping district. Of course her grandmother was quick to point out none of this was here when she was a young woman. Much of it had been built much later- some time after the war.

They wound their way through the narrow streets and parked

in front of a row house. Edward opened the door for them and assisted her grandmother out. Christine brought her luggage inside and laboured up the small, steep staircase. Her grandmother's cousin, Helen, showed her to a room at the top of the stairs where she and her mother would sleep for the next few days.

Helen had a fair complexion with warm, hazel eyes. Her Wigan accent was very similar to her grandmother's and made it easier to understand her fast paced manner of speaking. The aroma of lavender wafting off her clothing when she moved was very pleasant. Helen showed them the restroom on the second floor and the towels located in an armoire. Afterwards she disappeared back downstairs.

Christine felt badly for needing a nap but she knew she would need to rest a bit or face becoming ill. After staying awake all night she felt faint. She had always been the type of person who required a solid eight hours of sleep or she was useless. Her current state of exhaustion would make her cranky and ill-tempered to be around. Her mother, who followed her in, assured her no one would be upset with her and quietly shut the door behind her as she headed back downstairs. Alone in the small bedroom Christine made herself at home. She unzipped her suitcase, finding a large portrait of her fiance tucked inside. A small note accompanied it.

Dear Christine,

Have fun! I miss you already!

Jeff

She folded the note and tucked it in the side of her bag. She slipped into a comfortable nightshirt and lay down on the bed. Within minutes she fell fast asleep.

Hours later she awoke to the most wonderful aroma rising up the stairs. Outside there was no street noise or birds chirping as there had been earlier. Everything was oddly quiet. It was still light out but perhaps she'd slept much longer than she'd planned. She climbed out of bed and dressed in a pair of jeans and a knit top. She slipped on her boots and slowly descended the steep stairs, careful not to slip on the carpet. In the kitchen, Helen prepared a feast of something she called Bangers and Mash- and Mushy Peas. A quick peak in the cook pot and the large pans on the stovetop she realised the *bangers* were a type of sausage links, the *mash* were mashed potatoes and the *mushy peas* were just that- mushy peas. While Christine had never been much of a pea girl she had to admit they smelled quite wonderful. The house was quiet. Only Helen and Christine were at home.

"Your Mum and Grandmum have gone to visit her family's gravesite in Manchester. Her brothers had the headstones redone. You were sleeping so soundly they didn't want to trouble you."

"Is it far from here?"

"No, just around the corner. We'll need to take the car though. Would you like to see it as well?"

"I would."

"Then, eat your tea and I'll drive you there."

Christine smiled at the thought of *eating* her tea and then realised the evening meal itself was called 'tea'. She ate quickly, complimenting Helen on the meal. It was amazingly simple, but one of the tastier meals she'd ever eaten. After she finished, she ran upstairs to grab her jacket and scarf. She shoved some cash in her pocket and skipped back downstairs thankful she'd made a quick stop by the bank earlier in the week to change dollars for pounds. She left her Traveller's cheques packed figuring there was no need for those at a cemetery. A day for shopping would certainly arise on the trip but she seriously doubted it would be today.

Helen greeted her at the bottom. Her husband Gordon snoring in the family room.

"Don't mind him. He's always sleeping in front of the telly."

The graveyard was large and quite old. Some of the gravestones dated from hundreds of years earlier. It was late in the evening, and the low lying clouds turned into a misty fog and hung just above the ground. The cemetery was dank and cool, but not creepy in the least. There was a calm quiet to this particular graveyard. Christine never had cause to visit any graveyards back home. Both of her grandfathers died when she was a very young child. She had no recollection of the funerals or any of the events relating to their deaths. Visiting their headstones was something she'd had little involvement in throughout the years.

Her grandmothers, though both eighty years old now, were in exceptionally good health. One was an avid ballroom dancer and the other a power walker. As she walked the rows of the cemetery she realised she'd never even buried a friend. Her life was one filled with life- not loss.

She and Helen went in search of her mom and grandmother. They found them in the back corner of the lot kneeling in front of a monument in silent prayer. Her grandmother held a bouquet of silk flowers in her hands. She arranged them in the vase at the base of the granite stone. On the stone Christine found several names. Among them were the names of her great grandmother, Bessie, and her great grandfather. Next was the name of a girl, Elizabeth. Judging from the dates Elizabeth died as a young child and must of have been her grandmother's older sister. Below her name was James.

As if reading her thoughts, her grandmother explained about Elizabeth.

"Elizabeth was born two years before I was. She was seemingly healthy, but died in her sleep one night. Today we'd call it crib death but back then my mother couldn't understand it. It never happened to any of the women in our family prior to Elizabeth nor has it happened since. When I was born eighteen months later my mum worried over me day and night. She was fearful of the same thing happening again, but it didn't. God has a plan for each of us, though there were times I would've loved to have had an older sister around. That's why I was never bothered when your grandfather and I were blessed with four daughters.

I considered naming one of them after Elizabeth but never

did. My mother never wanted us to use the name again. She was worried it was unlucky or something. I of course didn't believe that but instead feel it was my sister's name and should remain that way. I named the girls after my four closest friends in England and their names suited them. Each one's personality shared some similarities to her namesake.

Through the years the girls were close. They had each other. The way they were born- the first two being closer in age and the younger two being closer in age- worked out perfectly. They always had each other to play with when they were little. As they grew older they were one another's' confidants and best friends. I can't take credit for planning it or anything. It's just the way it worked out. I would've been just as happy with four boys.

I often worried that your grandfather wanted a son, but he would just remark about how he was happy to have four healthy girls and sons wouldn't have brought him the same joy."

"I haven't really given any thought to children. I want them grandma but nowadays so many try to plan it out perfectly- I kind of figure when it happens it happens. My luck I'll have four boys. But like I said- I'll take it as it comes."

"Me too- we don't have much of a choice do we? You can plan many things in this lifetime, but children are like the weather- you could plan all you want but in the end it may rain! If it does you should be prepared but enjoy it nonetheless. Life would be boring without a little rain here and there."

"And dry!" Christine added.

Christine traced her fingers over James' name and the dates accompanying it. She wanted to ask about him. Her grandmother fondly called him by his nickname of Jimmy. She saw her grandmother watching her from the corner of her eye. She looked far off in the distance at an invisible place on the horizon.

"I wasn't there when Jimmy died." She confided. "I wanted to be but I wasn't. I felt cheated. He died while I still lived here in England, during the war. When I moved to the states I lost many friends and family members over the years. I was unable to attend their funerals due to distance and expense. It used to really trouble me, but it doesn't any more. Ray helped me to understand. He used to say the graves and funerals were for the living. The departed have already gone to their eternal resting place in heaven. So when I come to visit the gravesites like I'm doing today I try not to dwell on this part of it. They're up there- in heaven. Being at the funeral or gravesite isn't important. It's the memories we shared and the living we experienced which matters most. Remember this- someday when I'm gone."

Christine was glad to better understand her family's reasons for not visiting her grandfathers' graves more frequently. When Grandma explained it this way it all made perfect sense.

"I will remember. What happened to Jimmy, grandma? How did he pass?"

"You'll want to have a seat, Darling. This is a long story."

Her grandma walked over to a cement bench and took a seat leaving room for Christine to join her.

Chapter Eight

December 1942

A few weeks later, Kay received a letter from Jimmy. Its return post was Ward 2, Baguley Hosp. Kay, realizing it was from a hospital, sank down in the kitchen chair to read it.

Dear Sister and Brother,

May these few lines find you both fine and well, everything in Manchester being ok. I was transferred to the RAF Burtonwood in Warrington, Ches a few weeks back. I'm so close to home I hoped to surprise you on leave but now I fear it will be quite some time before that comes to pass. I have received some injuries to my upper body, shrapnel from an explosive. I am keeping pretty good at the moment

of writing this letter and slowly on the mend. I've been getting

around the ward a bit each day for exercise.

I must say the U.S. certainly looks after her servicemen and

so say all the Limey folks as the Yankee troops get the best of food

and good fillets. I saw a while back the G.I.'s meals at Burtonwood

camp- which sure made my mouth water when I thought of our

sparing diet. If I got the same G.I. meals now I think I'd be twice the

better for it as it's such first class food we need to fight, but never

mind things will improve in time.

May God bless and keep you Katie and little Anthony.

Brother Jimmy

"Whose the letter from?" Anthony broke her train of thought.

"Brother Jimmy. He's in hospital, not far from here actually."

"Is he well?"

"I can't tell."

"We must go see him."

"Yes, we must. I will tell Harry tomorrow and make the
arrangements."

Kay rose and slid her chair in.

Harry was an understanding and gentle man. Naturally he agreed to give them the day off. Kay had plenty of money for her railway fare as well as Anthony's. They were set to depart the following morning. The ride over was pleasant and shorter than expected.

"To think he's been so close by for the last few weeks and we knew not of it."

"Yes. War is a strange thing. The way they move them about. It is more difficult being those left behind. You spend all your time worrying about them. Praying for news, but only good news. Then when news finally comes you're afraid to open it."

"I'm sure he is well. We will know when we see for ourselves."

At the railway station they made their way to the hospital and located Ward 2. The nurse at the nurse's station smiled and directed them to Jimmy's room. They could hear him speaking with another man from outside the room. When they entered they saw the two of them were playing some sort of card game. Jimmy's entire upper torso was bandaged and blood tinged in a few places. The other man suffered from some sort of head wound. One eye was covered as well, but all in all they appeared in good spirits.

"Katie. Anthony. Is that you?"

"It is Jimmy."

Kay and Anthony went over to give him a light cuddle.

"You can hug me harder than that. I'm not going to break."

"It's just so good to see you." Kay looked him over and decided while he was hurt his wounds would heal in time.

"This is my mate, Matthew. We both served south of London together. He was moved to Burtonwood before me. Fancy us meeting up again here at hospital."

"It's nice to meet you."

Anthony shook Matthew's hand as well.

"How long until you come home?" Anthony asked.

"It may be a bit. Some of the metal cannot be removed- and well they have not cleared me to return to duty yet."

"I think he was hoping you'd receive a medical furlough as George did. Come home and stay for a few weeks." Kay clarified.

"We can hope can't we? We can hope." Jimmy ruffled Anthony's hair. "What news have you brought of Jonathan and Billie?"

"Jonathan is still in Scotland with the Sutherland Highlanders. I've brought his letters as well as those from Billie. Billie is working in the Home Guard on patrol. Last he wrote he was stationed near Dover." Kay handed Jimmy the stash of letters she stowed in her bag before leaving the house. "George and Billie saw each other quite frequently before. I'm guessing they still do. George married Theresa."

"I remember the girl. She was a stick the last I saw her but not to hear George tell it now."

"He speaks the truth Jimmy. She has grown quite beautiful these last two and a half years."

"I got to see both George and Billie from time to time in London. But it is Jonathan I've been bothered about."

"Well you needn't worry about him. I guess he's met a lovely Scottish gal there and intends to marry her."

"A Scottish gal? You don't say."

"Yes, I figured it best tell you this part of it now rather than risk injury to your heart when you discover it in his letters."

"We can't help who we love Katie though I'm sure father is rolling at the thought of a Scottish daughter."

"You never know. He'd mellowed with time."

"I'd say so. Age and time will do that to a man."

"We better get going." Kay spied the nurse standing just outside the doorway with a tray of meds. "Enjoy those letters Jimmy. I thought it might give you something to do in here- well something other than wooing the sweet nurses."

"Yes, there is always that. Anthony- take care of our Katie here. You are the man of the house now."

"I will Jimmy. Get well. I want to see you up and around before long."

"I hope to be."

Kay gave her brother a squeeze and felt the sting of tears burning her eyes. She held them back though. She must put on a brave face for him.

"God bless Jimmy."

Kay and Anthony closed the door. On the walk back to the railway station they were both unusually quiet.

"We can visit again, can't we?"

"Yes, Anthony we can. It took quite a bit of our savings to come here today. The war has made everything more expensive. I think if he is still in hospital in a month we'll have to come again."

"He looked poorly. Don't you agree?"

"Well- he's been injured. These things take time to heal."

What Kay left unsaid was he did look rather poorly- poorly indeed. His coloring was a mixture somewhere between ashen grey and yellow. His letter spoke of his 'sparing' diet. Was lack of nutrition the problem or was it something more grave? She knew he must have lost a lot of blood due to his injuries and then as a result of the surgeries as well. Shrapnel was not something she knew a whole lot about. He looked almost poisoned, from the inside out. What she had heard about shrapnel was it wasn't good. Not good at all.

At the train depot they boarded in silence. Anthony sat staring out the train window as they passed through the beautiful Cheshire countryside. Small cottages and farms dotted the landscape. The occasional burned out house or damaged hillside was visible as well, but all in all it appeared largely untouched by comparison to Manchester. Manchester suffered the casualties of a cruel, evil war. A war fought for perseverance and freedom. A war fought for liberty and happiness. The sacrifices of so many- and yet the war continued to cost them dearly.

The nightly air raids continued day after day. It became so commonplace if it hadn't been for young Anthony she wouldn't even bother leaving her room to seek shelter in the cellar. It seemed so certain. God had a plan. Either it was your time to go or it wasn't. Only he knew the answer to that question. Life continued on and Jimmy wrote Kay religiously. He told her second hand stories of Warrington and the G.I.'s who frequented there. Most of them were stationed in nearby Burtonwood and could easily make the less than two mile trip on foot.

Accounts of forced marriages and shabby goings on were all the gossip. It was no wonder Jimmy had a certain distaste for the Yanks- especially if one were to show interest in his sister. He repeatedly praised them in the war effort and described them as great mates but he clearly didn't want her dating one. Kay reassured him in her letters of her continued avoidance of the dances and other Yank infested hang-outs. This seemed to appease him.

One morning when Kay arrived at Harry's there was a nosegay of wild roses and daffodils on her work station and a box of chocolates. She whirled around expecting to find Jimmy had been released from the hospital and come home to surprise her- but he had not.

"Hello, Charlie. I told you I'd be back to visit in four weeks time."

"Oh."

"Well, don't look so disappointed!"

"I'm sorry, it's just I was expecting someone else."

"Oh, I see. Would this someone else be a man?"

"Yes, he would. Jimmy is his name."

"Jimmy. Sounds a bit boyish to me."

"You would say that. Thank you for the flowers and chocolates, but no thank you. You can take them back and give them to a more accommodating woman. From the looks of last month's dance I'm sure you won't have much difficulty in finding one."

He stepped closer to her and took her hand.

"Well, you see, therein lies the problem. The one I want doesn't want me and is pining away for someone else. Tell me about this Jimmy. I'm sure he is a swell chap."

"He certainly is. He is tall, much like you. He is handsome. Sandy blonde hair and light eyed like me." Kay decided whilst she was laying it on she might as well go all the way.

"Sounds like just about every other G.I. I know. What makes this one so special?"

"He has my heart."

"Well, it's hard to trump that."

"Then, there's the fact he isn't a G.I. at all. He is British."

"How long have you known him?"

"My entire life."

Well that was technically the truth.

"He's not your cousin or anything like that is he?"

"Nope. Not a cousin. That's something only your country does."

Still not a lie. He was not her cousin.

"Not only us. Let's not forget the British royal family. There are some married cousins in that family tree."

"Not that it matters. So as I was saying. Thank you for the flowers and chocolates, but I can't accept them. It would be insincere."

"Fine. I'll walk you home."

"But I just got here."

"But it's your birthday and I arranged for you to have the day off."

"My birthday?" Kay thought about it for a minute and realised it certainly was her birthday. "But how could you know that?"

"Jimmy told me."

"Jimmy?"

"Yes, your true love slash brother. He is a mate of mine and we only recently made the connection you were his sister. My Charlie is his Katie. Go figure."

"What a coincidence. Go figure. So Jimmy sent you to take me out for my birthday?"

"Not exactly but it is your birthday, isn't it?"

"It is."

"And you don't have any plans do you?"

"No. I guess not."

"Then, let's get out of here."

"So my brother doesn't know you're here?"

"He knows and let's just say I'm hoping he warms to the idea of us seeing each other."

"But I don't want to see you! Not dancing, dating or in any other capacity."

"So you keep telling me. Let me grab your jumper for you."

Ray gently draped her jumper over her shoulders.

Constance arrived to work and stopped short as Ray and Kay made their way out the front door.

"Happy Birthday, Kay! Hi Ray. Good to see you again."

"Good to see you too, Constance. Dick is in town."

"Fantastic. We'll see you both later."

Kay cast Constance a squinty eyed glance. Constance merely started humming as she strolled into the shop letting the door slam closed behind her.

"My brother has warned me against dating G.I.'s. I must advise you I don't expect him to change his opinion."

"He might. My intentions are good and I told him as much."

"We'll see. So what do you say we call a truce for now and you fill me in on our birthday plans."

"I've packed us a picnic lunch and stowed it in the park where Piggy is standing guard. Later there will be time for a quick change of clothing before we head out to the dance."

"This should be lovely. I have to spend the evening watching you twirling all too willing women around the dance floor. Sounds tempting."

"There is only one woman I'll be whirling around the dance floor. She is beautiful, petite, with an exceptionally feisty spirit and gorgeous gams. I've crossed the ocean to find her and I don't plan on letting her go." They'd stopped walking and were standing overlooking the park. "I'd already told you to save all your dances for me. I wasn't kidding."

"What makes you think I'll accept?"

"If not it will be a long miserable evening for us both. Suit yourself. I for one would rather spend it dancing with you."

"Hi Piggy. Did he put you up to this?"

"Sure did. We're all involved in this conquest in one way or another."

"A conquest. Interesting." Kay didn't like his choice of words.

Ray shot Piggy a cut throat look.

"Not a conquest. I'm not good with words." Piggy amended his previous statement.

"That's reassuring, Piggy."

"Yeah. Thanks a lot, Piggy."

Piggy left them alone and Ray opened the basket.

"We have cheese, bananas, grapes, crackers, wine, and a summer sausage."

"How did you get all these things?"

Kay's eyes grew wide in anticipation. She sorted through the items helping to lay them out on the blanket. She hadn't tasted cheese in two years. It had been even longer since she'd eaten grapes or bananas. Ray broke one off and handed it to her.

"I haven't eaten a banana in- a really long time."

"I figured." He opened the bottle of wine and poured some in a tin cup for her. Then did the same for himself. "Happy Birthday, Charlie. Let's make it a good one."

Kay sipped the wine, and then politely plucked a handful of grapes. She popped them into her mouth one at a time rather than pushing the whole lot of them into her mouth in one fistful as she'd like to have done.

"So what I can't figure is why me? You could obviously have your pick of girls and you're set on dating me. Why?"

"I don't want to date you. I want to marry you. The why is the easy part. You are different. You're sweet, yet incredibly strong. You're driven and resilient, yet incredibly feminine and beautiful. And I'm determined if I'm persistent enough you might just say yes."

"And maybe not. My brothers are all I've got. I'd never marry against their wishes- and then there's the other problem. I hardly know you. Meeting a man twice is not the makings of a solid marriage."

"They'll warm to me. You'll see."

"It really isn't that simple. You live far, far away. My home is here, in England."

"Nothing has to be decided today. Once you're madly in love with me we'll discuss logistics."

Ray leaned in and before Kay was the wiser he kissed her. It was a soft, sweet kiss which lasted entirely too long. Ronald Night and Pee-Pee were whistling from somewhere nearby. Ray rolled onto his back and put his hands behind his neck, resting his head on his hands. He gazed up into the sky.

"I'm sorry about those two fools."

Kay rolled onto her side and looked at him resting peacefully.

"Tell me about the war. What is it like doing what you do?"

"You really want to know?"

"I do."

"Well you know those bombers you see flying overhead- I do the same thing but for our side." Ray cringed as he spoke the words. "I'm proud to be a part of the US Army Air Force but when I enlisted I originally intended to be an aeroplane mechanic- would've preferred it actually. I've spent my entire life flying planes. For me it is a safe, happy place. I didn't want the burden of war to taint something I loved. I had all the necessary experience for both jobs but when I discovered Uncle Sam needed me as a pilot I acquiesced. Some might think it a glorious experience and it is, but at the same time…every day I fly a mission…I know I'm responsible for killing numerous people on the ground. No matter how often I tell myself they're the enemy and it is necessary, I still find it difficult to justify my role in the loss of life."

"What about your role in the preservation of life? Think of the countless lives you've protected by helping prevent invasion.

While war is about loss it is about victory as well. Victory over evil. Victory. This war will be remembered as when the great nations of the world came together in unity putting aside all differences to stand together. You have been an integral part of that. For this reason you should be proud."

"All things considered, we're all going to die sometime and I for one would rather die in a plane than anywhere…that's as close to heaven as you can get- unless of course I count this moment here with you." Ray reached over and held her hand where it lay on the blanket. "I'm going to survive this mess. The war will end and victory will be ours. I can imagine a time when I'll fly for the pure enjoyment of flying again."

"That's a nice thought. Thank you for sharing your story with me." Kay yawned feeling sleepy. "I think I'll take a rest as well." It'd been longer than she could recall since she'd had a full night's sleep let alone a nap, and while she should feel badly she didn't. She was tired and the cool air made her feel even sleepier. She closed her eyes. When she awoke a few hours later Ray was tickling her cheek with a daffodil.

"My flowers."

"Oh, so now you want them."

"I do."

Kay smiled sweetly at him.

"We better get going. There isn't much time to get changed for dinner and dancing."

They strolled home where Kay was greeted by Anthony and Edith who'd baked her a beautiful birthday cake. She celebrated with them and then ran upstairs to change. Tonight she would wear the purple frock given to her by Constance . She tried it on before and knew it would fit. A quick touch up to her make-up and hair and she was ready to go.

Ray awaited her at the bottom of the stairs. When she made her way to him he took her hand and this time she let him hold onto it. He winked at her.

"We work well together, Charlie."

"We'll see. So how is my brother looking these days?"

"Better. I've been taking him some steak once each week. We like to play cards. His roommate was from my unit. I'd met Matthew just before he was injured, then they ended up in the hospital at the same time. Roommates no less."

"He didn't look well when I was there last. I'm planning another trip over there to check on him."

"You might not need to. I expect they'll release him in a week or so. He really is almost in A1 shape. That's what he says anyhow."

"Sounds like him. If he's not released this week I'm going back."

"Okay. I won't try to convince you otherwise."

"Yes. That'd prove futile."

At the dance all of her girlfriends were there dancing the night away. Susan was on the arm of a Canadian G.I. The other girls seemed angry with her. She made no effort to speak with them and they snubbed her in return. Kay knew something was amiss but couldn't figure out what. When she saw her walk outside unattended she decided to go after her.

Outside Susan stood smoking alone. She stared off into the distance and was distracted. She didn't seem to notice Kay's soft approach.

"Susan. How have you been keeping?"

"So I see you're still speaking to me."

"Why wouldn't I be?"

"I had a row with Constance. She's cross with me."

"I must admit to noticing something was about but I couldn't figure out what. I followed you out to check on you. Make sure you're all right."

"Well, I am. They think I should be spending more time at home. I may be married but I'm not dead. I'm only twenty-two after all, hardly an old woman. I want to go out dancing and have fun- and why shouldn't I?"

"I guess there is no harm in dancing."

"Certainly not. I will not let them bully me into sitting at home wasting my youthful years. This bloody war could drag on forever! For all I know he may get killed! And I'll be here alone!"

Susan threw down her cigarette and ran off down the lane. Kay called to her but she made no attempt to stop. Kay walked back into the hall. Ray met her at the door.

"Everything okay?"

"Yes. Let's go dance."

Kay knew she should let it alone but she couldn't help but be concerned. When Ray and his buddies went for a smoke outside she opened up to Constance about Susan.

"Dancing? Is that what she called it?"

"Yes- actually she did."

"Well, it's not the dancing or the drinking we're all worried about. I told her as much. It's the repeated overnight visits with multiple men. She's a married woman! She should behave like one. I told her if she's not careful she'll wind up pregnant! That's a situation no woman should get herself into- especially one who is already married! Running around on him is bad enough, but if she goes and gets pregnant with another man's baby- can you imagine? Everyone has seen her! They will tell him when he returns home. She is daft."

Constance looked as if she would burst into tears. Dick walked up. Constance excused herself claiming she had a headache and wanted to lie down. He offered to walk her home. They left, his arm slung loosely around her shoulders.

Kay stood stunned for a few moments. Susan and Constance were both so completely out of sorts. Both seemed incredibly stressed by their fight. Kay decided to leave well enough alone and finished her evening in Ray's arms twirling about the dance floor.

Suffice to say, it was the best night she'd spent out in years.

Chapter Nine

March 1943

Several weeks passed and Jimmy continued sending letters.

He sounded well and upbeat. They visited him again and this time he

looked much improved. More weeks passed and more letters arrived.

Kay had high hopes of him being released. In October, Kay spoke of

making another visit. When he received the letter detailing her plans

he rang Martha's house next door, leaving a message for Kay to

return his call. Martha's house held the only working phone on her

street and as her neighbour she allowed Kay the privilege of

receiving and making calls there.

Kay returned Jimmy's call and was pleasantly surprised of the progress he was making. He convinced her to cancel her trip insisting he'd be out before she could get there. Then one day in November she received a message from Ray she must come to Warrington right away. She decided to take Anthony with her, knowing the situation with Jimmy must be dire.

The first available departure to Warrington was in the morning. They would depart at seven o'clock, arriving sometime before eleven. Kay hadn't booked a return not knowing how long they'd need to be gone. She spoke with both Harry and the plant manager before leaving work. Both said to stay as long as need be. That night Kay prayed for her brother, for the unknown. She had no idea what could have happened to make him take this sudden turn. One moment he was well, writing letters of his progress and the next she was travelling to his bedside prepared for the worst. The night was a fitful one.

She tossed and turned, the sirens sounded endlessly outside and the air raid seemed to last interminably. By five o'clock in the morning she decided any attempt at sleep was fruitless, and made her way to the kitchen.

"Couldn't sleep either?"

Anthony sat in the dark of their small sitting room in their mother's old rocker, covered with her quilt.

"No."

"I just don't understand what happened. He seemed so well when we last visited. Better than the first visit- stronger, better color. I don't understand."

"Me neither. It will all work out." But even as Kay spoke the words she was unsure. A knock came at their door.

Kay stared at the door, unable to force herself to stand to answer it. The rap came again, louder this time. Anthony rose and walked over to open it. He patted Kay's knee as he walked through the kitchen and opened the door to a teary eyed Martha.

"A call just came from the charge nurse at hospital in Warrington. Jimmy's died around three o'clock this morning. I'm truly sorry for your loss."

"Thank you, Martha. Thank you for bringing word."

Anthony closed the door and knelt where he stood in the kitchen.

"I hate this bloody war. I hate every aspect about it. The

Germans. They're beasts, savage beasts and murderers. I can't wait until I'm nineteen. I'll show them. I'll kill every single last one of them I can find."

Kay walked over to her brother and knelt behind him placing her hand on his shoulder.

"Don't say such things, Anthony. Don't you think we all hate the war? Don't you think we're all praying it'll end soon?"

"Why Jimmy? He was so young. Only twenty-one. He'd never been with a woman! He'll never marry. He'll never have children of his own. It's not fair Katie! It's not bloody fair!"

"War is never just. It is never kind or pleasant. It is ugly and cruel. I hate what it has done to our lovely Britain. I hate it. The war has stolen Mum from us and now Jimmy, but we must go on. For Jonathan, Billie and George. They're still out there and they're depending on us to be strong for them. I will send word to them immediately."

Anthony brushed past her into the front garden and out onto the street, disappearing at a fast clip. Kay walked next door to Martha's. She tapped lightly on the door. Martha opened it and warmly embraced her.

"I've put the kettle on for tea. I've made breakfast as well. Where's Anthony?"

"He's gone for a walk."

"It's just as well he did. Would you like to use the phone?"

"I would, thank you."

Kay called the numbers for each of her brothers they had sent her. Each of the contacts promised to get a message to them as quickly as possible. Of course they'd be unable to attend the funeral but they'd want to know just the same.

"Are you still going to go to Warrington this morning?" Martha asked pouring them each a cup of tea.

"I don't see the point now."

"No, I guess you're right."

Kay finished her tea and breakfast. She walked back to her home and found Edith was hard at work in the kitchen preparing meat dumplings.

"You've heard about our Jimmy?"

"Yes, just. I'm very sorry."

"Thank you. I'll finish those if you'd like. Maybe you'd like to go find Anthony and fetch him home?"

"I don't know if he wants to see me right now. We've had a bit of a quarrel and he's sore with me."

"Can't be that bad, go on and find him."

Edith took off her pinny and handed it to Kay .

Kay cooked in silence and was thankful for it. Most of the other women worked the second and third shifts at Harry's and were still sleeping soundly. Kay rolled out the dough for her dumplings and carefully cut it into triangles. She chopped the meat into small bits and mixed it with a sprinkle of flour, parsley and potato. She learned to make meat dumplings with her mother around ten years of age and had perfected the technique since then- her short stint at the pastry shop making meat pies expanding her abilities.

Tears rolled down her cheeks and fell in large drops on the collar of her shirt. What started out as silent tears erupted in violent sobs.

How many more will be claimed before this all ends? Will I lose them all?

She took the knife she was using and repeatedly stabbed the small piece of horse roast, again and again. She stabbed it until the knife became stuck in the wood cutting board. Arms came around her from behind. Warm arms she recognised as Ray's. He held her, whispering in her ear.

"Let it all out, just let it all out. I'm here with you now and it will all be okay."

Kay turned and laid her head on his shoulder and cried until her tears dried and there weren't any more. Ray scooped her up and took her upstairs where he laid her across her bed and covered her legs against the November chill. He cuddled up behind her and held her until she slept. He must have snuck out at some point because when she awoke he was gone. She crept out of bed and tiptoed downstairs drawn by the sounds of laughter, and something marvellous wafting up from the kitchen.

In her kitchen she found Edith, Anthony, and Ray all around the table playing some foolish game which involved pints of beer, cards and bets. It was good to see Anthony smiling. He and Edith obviously ended their spat. Edith occupied his lap and his arms were wrapped lazily around her waist.

He'd lost his mother at fourteen and since then there'd been no man in his life. Maybe now would be a good time for a man to man- or brother to sister chat as the case may be. Ray looked at her and winked.

"Looks like it might be a good time to add another player to the game."

"She's not a heavy drinker. I must warn you. One drink and she's snockered."

"I wouldn't mind seeing that." Ray teased. "Come sit with me."

Kay took a seat on his knee.

"How do I play?"

"Game's called Pontoon. It's simple- just watch and learn."

Kay watched the remainder of the game and after an hour she was prepared to try her hand at it. She glanced across the table at Anthony. He seemed happy considering the drab situation they found themselves in. In a few days' time they would bury a brother and add him to the growing number of casualties. It was another loss, not only for Jolly Old England, but for their small family. There were five of them left now. Kay, Anthony, George, Jonathan and Billie. They were spread apart, separated by space and limited communications during this dreadful war. Kay was filled with a new determination. A determination focused on solely keeping what was left of her family together.

One more year and Anthony would be nineteen. Like all the rest of them he'd be called into service for his country. Kay dreaded the day but knew it would come. This war appeared to be endless and Kay felt helpless in her ability to change that. She'd have to do what she could. She decided she would do a better job at writing to her brothers. While she'd done a wonderful job at penning letters to Jimmy, she hadn't posted letters to the others in a few months. She set a goal of sending a letter to each of them every week. She would focus her energies on spending more time with the one she had at home. She needed to live- truly live. During the past few years she'd filled her life with work, keeping her mind and heart busy in order to avoid worry.

She thought back to Jimmy's letter about the poor food available to him. About the food the G.I.'s received. She hated the fact her other brothers were possibly experiencing the same thing. Poor rations- a sparing diet as Jimmy had called it. To look on as the others had good food, better food. It saddened her deeply. She knew she needed to do something about it, but wasn't sure how to go about it. She didn't have the power or the authority to change the rations or availability of food throughout all of Europe for the British troops, but she could certainly make an effort where her own brothers were concerned. Many times she'd longed to send them something special, but there just wasn't much available. Sticks of chewing gum taped inside her letters had been all she was able to accomplish. She knew her brothers greatly appreciated it as each of them mentioned the gum and looking forward to receiving it. But what more could she do? Certainly she could do better than a couple of sticks of gum.

The game finished and Edith led Anthony to the sitting room.

"What are you thinking about, Charlie?"

"My brothers. The four remaining. The chocolates you brought me for my birthday. Are they easy for you to get?"

Kay knew for her the chocolates would be nearly impossible to buy. Things such as chocolates, candies, stockings and such were only available if you knew a G.I. who got them for you.

"Relatively. Why?"

"I'd like to start putting together one package each week for my brothers."

"A sort of care package?"

"Yes. And then I'll rotate through each brother. One each

week, four weeks in a month. That sort of thing."

"I can get you chocolates, cigarettes and small packages of coffee."

"Wonderful! I just wish we could do it for more of them."

"Maybe we can. I'm sure I could get some of the other men to donate- if they're not currently using all of their treats to woo British girls."

"Yes, Jimmy warned me of their exploits in Warrington. Assembling in the town square and luring young women to ride in their vehicles. I've even heard about young women disappearing and the sudden appearance of much younger siblings upon their return."

"Unfortunately such reports are true which is why I'm hiding out in Manchester on my leaves. I've got something here to keep me out of trouble."

Ignoring his comment Kay continued detailing her plan.

"So if we could get eight chocolate bars, small bags of candy and coffee, we could set a goal of my brothers plus four. This would be a good starting point."

"I think you're underestimating the American troops. You'll be surprised at what rolls in. We may like British women, but we're quite a giving bunch."

Within days Kay's house became a staging area for all of the donated items. She couldn't believe what lined her small dining room walls. Small cans of condensed milk, chocolates in every shape and size, coffee, tea and small cans of meat as well. It was truly amazing what word of mouth could provide. She and her housemates worked tirelessly to put together the care packages and sent them to military camps in Scotland, Ireland and throughout England. Just when supplies began to run low a large convoy rolled through town stopping off to deliver even more. Kay was touched by this outpouring of love in a time when there was so much sadness. Within weeks, thank you letters from British servicemen all over Europe flowed in.

The lulls between Ray's visits widened as the war and the need for more missions as a pilot heightened. One particular Friday evening Kay sat awaiting his arrival. They'd planned it for weeks. As the hours ticked past Kay became increasingly alarmed. By midnight she surmised he wasn't coming. He'd been detained for whatever reason. She went to sleep. The following morning she awoke at dawn and walked down to Martha's house to check for a message but there was none. As each day passed, her anger and initial annoyance gave way to fear.

No message. No letter. No telegram.

Where could he be? What must have happened?

Kay continued on going about her business. She had little other choice. In her opinion the burden of this awful war was the woman's to suffer- alone. They must remain behind. Wondering about their loved ones- fearing the worst and praying at all times for the best. Hanging on to every notice, searching the names for loved ones and sending out condolences for friends who'd heard about a devastating loss. Day after day was spent the same way. Worry filled days, weeks and months.

Finally, Kay arrived after work over a week later to find Ray sitting on her front steps. He looked horrid- tired and his face haggard. He seemed as if he hadn't slept in days. Regardless of his heavily burdened appearance, Kay was both angry and relieved to see him. Relieved he was alive and well. Angry that he was both alive and well- and hadn't bothered to ring her!

"Hello, Charlie."

"Don't hello Charlie me. I thought you were dead or

something."

"Not dead, just exhausted."

"You do have a phone somewhere on that camp. You've phoned before. Don't pretend you don't know how to use it."

"I couldn't have rung your neighbour's house in the middle of the night. To wake someone for something other than an emergency wouldn't be right."

"So you expect me to believe you've been working around the clock for nearly nine days."

"Yes, it's the truth. When I've not been flying I've been sleeping what little I can. Some nights getting fewer than four hours. I've been in the air mostly flying back to back missions."

"You should've called and you know it. You can try to use that two bit excuse on an American girl but it won't work on me."

She walked passed him and into the house. The warm days of spring brought with them the sweet smell of wild roses and daffodils growing in the gardens once more. Kay and the few other neighbours on her street replanted their gardens as best they could and everything began to bloom. Even an apple tree across the way survived the ongoing air raids and was covered in sweet blossoms.

Kay left both front and back doors propped open to create better air circulation. The end result was the sweet aroma of spring throughout the house.

Kay worked in the kitchen making tea when she saw a hat sail through the front door and come to a skidding halt just past the kitchen. She walked over and looked at it. It was Ray's. She picked it up and threw it right back out the front door.

An hour later his hat skidded back in through the front door and halted once more in the kitchen. Kay walked back over to it and tossed it back out the front door. Another hour passed and Anthony walked into the house, a sullen Ray on his heels.

"Look what I found outside."

"If he is coming inside it is as your guest, not mine."

"Come on guest o' mine, Ray. Let's have tea. Have you met my lovely, even tempered sister Katie before?"

Kay threw a kitchen towel at her brother and stomped from the room.

"She's angry with you mate. I dunno if you can fix that."

The men ate and started playing a game of poker. A while later Kay appeared back downstairs, dressed in a bright yellow frock and waist coat. She wore a hat and her hair was neatly curled. She walked right through the kitchen and out the front door without a word to either of them. It didn't take long for Ray to come running.

"Where are you headed?"

"There's a camp dance tonight and Constance asked me to attend. I've decided it might be a good idea."

"Oh, you have."

"Yes. I'm sure there is some G.I. there who won't mind jitterbugging the night away with me."

"Come on, Charlie. You can't stay angry."

"You'd be surprised."

"Fine, but don't do anything you can't take back."

Kay walked ahead of him to where Constance waited on the corner.

"You two have a fight?"

"Let's just say after tonight he'll ring if he can't make it."

"I'll make sure you have no shortage of dance partners."

The two winked conspiratorially and linked arms. At the dance a few hours later, Kay danced with every G.I. who asked her. Ray's friends stood at a corner table watching her closely. She scanned the room for him and could see he was nowhere around. The night slipped by and Kay cut a rug with every man in the room who possessed an ounce of rhythm and even a few who didn't. The last slow song played signaling an end to the evening and the lights came on. Constance and Kay made the journey home. Dick and Piggy escorted them home.

"Ray put you up to this?"

"Maybe he did, maybe he didn't."

Back at her house a sloshed Ray was leaning against the front door.

"Anthony took me to the men's club. Then he told me I could wait up for you out here."

"How long you going to make him suffer Kay?" Dick asked sounding pitiful.

"You did dance with every man there. Isn't that punishment enough?" Ray slurred, stumbling to his feet.

"Good night you two." Constance, Dick, and Piggy headed off towards her house, the three of them linking arms as they went.

"You saw that? Well good."

Kay walked inside and left the door open behind her.

Moments later a hat sailed in through the front door and landed near the kitchen table. She picked it up, popped it on her head and walked back over to the door.

"Yes, you can come in."

"Thank goodness. My backside is sore from this stone step."

Ray wrapped his arms around her and kissed her long and deep.

"Marry me, Charlie. I don't think I can stand another evening of watching you dance with other men."

"Don't disappear on me and you won't have to."

"You haven't answered my question yet."

"I'll think about it, Ray. I'll think about it."

"That's better than a no."

Kay locked the front door and walked to the living room handing Ray a blanket and a pillow.

"You can sleep on the settee."

"I'm just thankful to be inside and off the stoop."

Kay bent to kiss him good night, covered him and tucked him in.

"See you in the morning."

"Or maybe sometime in the middle of the night."

"You wouldn't dare."

"I was referring to the air raid, but that doesn't sound half bad either."

Kay blushed fiercely. She turned and walked up the stairs. She slept soundly until the sirens. She sat up and Ray was there beside her, extending his hand to her. They walked hand in hand into the cellar to join the others. They sat on one of the cots and chatted until dawn. Kay shared with him her dreams of owning her own bakery. He shared with her his dreams of working for a large airport as a mechanic, as well as owning his own small plane.

They both shared the dream of a post-war Europe where peace reigned and children returned to the streets of Manchester. A time when air raids never woke you in the middle of the night and families weren't separated. A time when storefronts were full of the finest dresses and clothing and grocers had everything you wanted to buy. Kay longed to drink sweet cream and eat her fill of steak. She wanted to sink her teeth into a strawberry or even an orange. What she wouldn't do for a glass of orange juice.

So they sat and made plans for a future. A future free of war.

Later the following morning, as Ray stood in the bathroom shaving, Kay tucked a small note in the pocket of his trousers. It merely read...

The answer is Yes. Be safe. God bless. Xoxo Charlie

#

Christine linked arms with her mother and grandmother. The sun was setting as they arrived back at Helen's car. Helen cranked the engine and they made the short trip home to her house. Later during the night Christine thought about her grandparents. Amid war and devastation they found love. Extreme circumstances brought them together, bridging an ocean. Compared with theirs, she thought her own love story seemed simple.

She and Jeff met in college. He'd been the teacher's assistant in her French Lit class. One day after class when Christine stopped by Professor Archambeau's office to inquire about the best French-English dictionary to purchase for translation purposes- well there he was. He spoke French much better than she did. It didn't take long to learn why. He was born in Quebec- his parents immigrated to Illinois for his father's job when he was only six. Jeff started elementary school there and after high school moved to Florida where he attended college.

Within weeks of meeting her, Jeff swept Christine off her feet. He wrote her love letters and poems in French- some of which she could barely read. He packed picnic lunches and took her for drives in the countryside. He made her feel special and comfortable, but most importantly he treated her like a lady. Christine contemplated their love story. Maybe she'd be sharing it with her granddaughter someday retracing their college days in Florida.

The following morning was a rainy one, quite typical of weather in Wigan this time of year. Christine and her grandmother donned rain coats and carried umbrellas as they strolled into town. Along the way they passed a dress shop and decided to stop in. There was a large variety of mostly formal dresses crowding the small shop. It was difficult to browse what was there due to the enormous quantity of dresses pressed onto each rack.

At the back of the shop there was a rack of bridal gowns marked as clearance. The shopkeeper approached them explaining how she'd picked them up from another shop that had gone out of business. Christine checked the prices and found they were truly quite reasonably priced. Her grandmother insisted she try one on.

Even if it needed altering a dress bought on their trip to England would be quite a unique find.

Christine couldn't have agreed more and had no trouble finding four she would like to see on herself. One was strapless with a tightly fitted bodice adorned with sequins and pearls. Its long, flowing skirt sported a large bow at the back. It was off white and quite stunning- her grandmother couldn't have agreed more. Christine told her about her fruitless shopping trips to numerous malls in Central Florida and one ill-fated trip to a Tampa wedding dress shop where the only thing she found was a veil she liked. She'd returned empty handed and a little down.

Today was entirely different. This dress fit like it was made for her. While she never really considered herself a fan of bows- this dress was unique. The bow was tastefully done and added a degree of elegance to the back of the dress. Christine liked the dress so much she didn't need to even try the others.

"I'll take it!" She announced.

"Get changed, dear. I'll see about having it shipped."

Moments later when Christine stepped out of the changing room her grandmother stood smiling at the register. The dress was neatly packed in a garment bag and draped over her arm.

"You ready?"

"I just need to pay for it first."

"Already taken care of."

Christine rushed over and embraced her grandmother.

"Thanks, Grandma!"

"You're welcome- now let's go see about shipping it back home. There's a post office just around the corner according the clerk. It shouldn't take much to ship it off today and have it there when you get back."

"Good. I'll ring Vanessa and let her know she'll need to sign for it."

"Perfect. Afterwards we can grab lunch."

Outside it looked as if the drizzling rain was here to stay.

"I'll tell you one thing- I sure haven't missed this weather. Give me that good old Florida sunshine any day of the week!"

"Is it always this dreary?"

"I thought all the world was until your grandfather married me and brought me to the United States. I became a beach goer very quickly."

"Some things never change, I guess. I was wondering what your wedding dress looked like?"

"Mine? Well we made it of course."

Chapter Ten

January 1944

That winter was a cold one and with there being little else to do other than work and bundling up inside, Kay, Constance, Theresa, and Edith began a new project sewing Kay's bridal gown. The four women worked endlessly after work each day to hand stitch the beautiful white gown. The fabric was a gift from Harry and was heavy satin. The girls had enormous plans for this dress and even with them all sewing it would take several months to complete. The dress would have an ornate train complete with beadwork and pearls. The bodice would be trimmed in lace, which they didn't have yet and had no idea where it would come from. Kay wanted to wear a full veil and the lace for it would be expensive as well as difficult to find. Regardless, the girls took Kay's measurements and forged onward.

The war raged on and things were the way they'd been for the last three years. Kay began to wonder if the cold weather, drab meals, and endless war would be her life- forever. The prospect of wedded bliss was all which kept the girls moving ahead. Ray was moved from Warrington to Suffolk. He was farther away now and this made their visits much more challenging. Kay saw him once every three months and it wasn't nearly frequent enough. Still she held her head high and continued the efforts of care packages and sewing parachutes. She couldn't allow him to see her cry or saddened. So every three months she met him with a smile and a kiss, making the most of every moment.

She'd filed all the necessary paperwork for their marriage licence as well as made arrangements for their wedding announcement to run in the bands for the church. Marriages were required to be announced for so many weeks in a row prior to the wedding date if you wanted to wed in the Catholic Church. This required time and planning, and while a war waged around them, the traditional practises of the church continued. The local priest made exceptions for no one.

Kay sat with Edith sipping tea and doing beadwork in the late evening when a knock came at the door. It was Constance.

"Come in."

Constance came in and stood with water dripping off her. The cold rains continued and snow was forecast for tomorrow. It was on days like these thoughts of her brothers, possibly weathering the frigid storms outside somewhere, plagued her mind. Constance stood just inside the doorway, teeth chattering and drenched. She made no move to come in and sit down.

"What's the matter? You'll catch your death standing there soaked to the bone. Please come in. Edith, please go grab her a towel."

"Maybe I will catch my death. Anything would be better than living in this hell."

"Don't say such things."

"I've done something awful, Kay. Something dreadfully awful."

"You know no matter what it is I will love you the same. Nothing could make me feel otherwise."

"I'm expecting a child, Kay. Dick's child."

Kay thought back to their conversation months before about Susan and wondered how far along Constance was.

"Have you told him?"

"I'd planned on telling him when they came for a visit next month, but then I received this letter today."

She handed a letter to Kay. Kay took the letter and pulled it from the wet envelope.

Dear Constance,

Writing this letter to you is one of the most upsetting things I've ever had to do. I'm Dick's wife of ten years. Recently he wrote to me and confessed all about his ongoing affair with you. As a good woman- and I know you are for he has said so- I beg of you not to see him anymore.

He is in love with you and told me as much, but as his wife I must tell you how much he means to me and to our two children. I understand and forgive you both this indiscretion as I can't imagine how lonely he has been these past few years. He has confessed you knew nothing of us and for that I'm truly sorry. He is a wonderful, loving man and I know how devastating this news must be in reaching you.

He has every intention of telling you himself on his next leave, but from one lady to another I felt compelled to tell you first. He has asked me for a divorce and wishes to be with you after the war and if it were only myself I had to consider- well that would be different. The children and my commitment to home and my marriage vow must be my excuse. You see- I cannot let him go without a fight. I feel the war and the distance between us may have confused him. I'm asking you to allow me the opportunity to set things straight between us.

I hope and pray this war will bring him safely home to us, at which time I'll be able to reaffirm the relationship we had before. Wishing you all the best and wanting nothing more for you than health and happiness, please understand my plea.

Sincerely,

Margarette

"So he has never spoken of his wife and children to you?"

"No, he hasn't. This is the first I'm hearing of them."

Kay stood to grab the towel and dry clothing Edith brought from her bedroom upstairs. Kay looked at Constance not sure whether she wanted Edith to know about her situation.

"Please have a seat with us, Edith. There is no use in keeping this a secret. Everyone will know soon enough. I'm expecting. Nearly five months along."

"Oh."

Poor Edith was at a loss for words, merely plopping down on the sofa.

"Well, that's one way to look at it."

Constance handed her the letter as well. After Edith finished reading it, she set it down on the table.

"What are you going to do?"

"I've told my mum and dad. While they were a little bothered by it, I am their only child and my mum has always felt a baby's a blessing no matter what the circumstances. I'm grateful for that. As for Dick, I plan on telling him in two weeks' time when he visits next- he certainly has a right to know. Beyond that I plan not to see him again. She has asked me not to…I must respect her request."

"But you're having his child, too." Edith spoke.

"I am, but she is his wife and mother to two of his children. I never would've gotten involved with a married man if I'd known the truth. As for the baby- I won't deny him access to visiting the baby or a relationship if he wants one with the baby either."

"You've borne this well, Constance . I don't know I could have done as well as you are doing. This baby will certainly have no shortage of doting aunties."

"Thank you, Kay ."

"You know, we've accomplished quite a bit on my dress and we don't have the lace to complete it anyhow. Why don't we put it on hold for a while and begin preparations for the baby? I could sew a quilt." While Kay's dress was certainly nowhere near being completed, she decided a white lie just this once would be okay. Her friend needed her support and making the baby cause for celebration by sewing a quilt would be just the thing she needed.

"I could make some baby clothes. I made some for my cousin once and it was quite fun." Edith offered.

Tears streamed down Constance's face.

"Thank you, both."

"It will all work out for the best, you'll see." Kay wore a

smile but deep down she was seething. Ray and the others must have known Dick was married. Why hadn't anyone told Constance the truth? She and her broken heart would be just another casualty of this hideous war. She wasn't the only girl to find herself in this situation. Kay heard the horrid tales of many others. The G.I.'s who were married and behaved in such a manner should be ashamed of themselves.

The days crawled by until Ray and his friends were scheduled to visit. Constance was frightfully sick each day at work and left her work station in order to be sick in the restroom. All of the girls agreed to keep the secret from Harry as to not endanger Constance's job. By day five of her illness they were all quite sure even Harry sussed it out but he said nothing. Instead of firing her or asking her to take a leave he seemed more inclined to baby her. He brought her dry toast and tea to settle her stomach. He even offered her longer than normal breaks and lunches.

The door to the shop opened around four o'clock in the afternoon. It was Ray and Dick. They each carried a bouquet of wild roses in hand. Utter silence fell over the workplace as the women all greeted Dick with icy stares. He'd have to be dumb not to have noticed. Constance stood and coolly smiled at him taking the flowers.

"Would you care to join me for a stroll outside?"

Harry came over and brushed past Dick knocking his shoulder as he passed by.

"Sure."

Constance led the way outside.

"I'll be off at five. Thanks for the flowers." Kay stood on tiptoe to kiss Ray's cheek.

"Okay. I'll see you then."

After Ray left the shop Veronica, Theresa, and Hilda all looked over at Kay. Hilda muttered under her breath.

"Wish we were still sewing trousers. I might be able to sew a special pair for the likes of him. Ones with needles still hidden in the crotch."

The room erupted in laughter.

"Odious man. A wife and kids at home, a young pregnant girlfriend overseas."

"He's betrayed the whole lot of them. Even if he divorced his wife and married Constance - she could never trust him. Not fully."

"She knows that. She's brighter than that."

Moments later Constance came back into the shop, head held high.

"So?"

"He knows about the baby. He knows about his wife's letter- she wrote him advising him she'd done it. There's nothing more to say. I don't know if he'll want a relationship with the baby. Let's get back to work."

Constance sat at her work station and worked diligently. Following her lead everyone set to work without another word. When the clock sounded five o'clock, Kay caught her bus alone and headed for home. Constance and Veronica opted to walk home.

Ray was sitting on the steps as usual and stood to hug Kay.

"I've heard about Dick and Constance - just."

"Did you know he was married?"

"No. He never spoke of his wife. When he was first assigned to our camp I'd already been here six months. I haven't known him any longer than all of you. He told me the truth last week. Of course none of us knew Constance was expecting at that time."

"What is he going to do?"

"Nothing. Constance has made it clear she wants nothing to do with him."

"She is hurt and embarrassed. Humiliated to have received such a letter from a wife she knew nothing about. It is a difficult situation."

"Certainly is. He is willing to leave his wife for her but she won't hear of it."

"Certainly not. Then there would be a ruined family and two children left fatherless."

"I don't know that there is a right or wrong answer in this situation."

"Only a man would say such a thing. Of course there is a right and a wrong answer in this situation. He should never have dated a young woman when he was married in the first place! Didn't he know this would be a possibility? That she could end up pregnant?"

Ray held his hands up.

"Truce! I'm not the enemy here. I'm just as upset by all of this as you are. I can't imagine what Constance is feeling now. I can't imagine the fear of having a baby in the middle of this chaotic war. She must be terrified."

"If she is- she is doing a good job of covering, but she still has four months before the baby will arrive."

"Late October."

"Yes."

"Well, on a more positive note my mother sent you this package."

Ray reached under the table where he'd stowed a medium sized box. Kay opened it. Inside there were various widths of white lace. Rolls and rolls of it ranging from quarter inch to twelve inch. There was enough to trim the bodice of her gown and make the veil as well. Maybe even enough left over for a Christening gown for the Constance's baby.

"It's beautiful. How did she know?"

"I sent her a letter announcing our engagement and the shortage of lace- she sent this. It arrived earlier this week. I forwarded it here where Anthony stowed it safely beneath the table."

"It's been here all week?"

"Sure has. Pull it all out. Let's look it over."

As Kay pulled the lace out, she laid it all out on the table, according to size. At the bottom there was a small package wrapped in brown paper. On it there was a handwritten note.

For Kay's wedding day. Love Ma

"What's this?"

"I don't know. Open it and see."

She unwrapped it and a pair of silk nylons fell onto her lap. She picked them up and gently ran her hands over them. She hadn't owned a pair since the war began. Her mother owned a few pairs that were filled with runs and snags. Kay tried them on once in hopes she could make do with a pair of them but they were too worn. She ended up throwing them all away. Now she would have a pair of her very own for her wedding day. There was a lace handkerchief trimmed in tatted lace as well. The flower detailing of the tatting design was exquisite.

"She asked me in her corresponding letter when the wedding would be. So when will it be Charlie?"

"I was hoping for summer of next year. June 1945. It has such a nice sound to it."

"June 1945. I think summer will be perfect."

"Thank you for writing your mum about the lace and the

stockings. They're more than I'd ever expected. I'll write her a thank you tomorrow."

"She'd love a letter from you. Come on- let's go fit me for a suit. I'll need one for our wedding."

"But it's more than a year off!"

Ray led her upstairs to the room which held her sewing box and measuring tape.

"Yes- but I think I'll enjoy getting measured by you. Besides- we'll need fabric and mother wants to know how much to send, color and weight. I don't know any of those details so I need you to get measurements for me."

"And that's all you'll be getting, sir."

"A man can hope can't he?"

"Watch it, Ray! I'll be armed with stick pens and a measuring tape!"

Kay took all of the measurements and jotted them down. She spoke while she worked.

"Does your mother sew?"

"A lot. She was quite saddened she couldn't be here to help with your gown. I wouldn't be surprised to find out she is working on something of her own back in North Brookfield right this very minute."

"I wonder what."

"I think she mentioned a Christening gown."

"For a baby!" It was one thing to consider sewing one for Constance who was really expecting, but an entirely different idea to sew one for herself. Kay nearly fell backwards.

"Yes for a baby. What else?"

"We aren't even married yet."

"I know but I think she figures once we are a baby won't be far behind."

"Maybe not."

"You do want children, don't you Charlie?"

"Of course. It's just it's difficult right now to imagine bringing any child into a world filled with air raids and such. I can't imagine anything beyond this blasted war."

"In time. It is going to end soon. I have faith in that. Have you given any thought to a move to the United States?"

"I have. My brothers aren't thrilled, but they know you were a mate of Jimmy's and it goes a long ways with them. They're all looking forward to meeting you someday. All done with the measurements."

"Perfect."

Kay went downstairs to wait for him. Moments later he came down carrying a folded piece of paper.

"I brought you something else. I started writing our song. If you had a guitar I'd play it for you, but since you don't I'll sing the chorus."

Kay came over and kissed him sweetly. Ray produced a gold necklace with a heart shaped locket from his shirt pocket.

"Since you said yes this belongs to you."

He clasped it around her neck and hugged her gently.

Chapter Eleven

In early June, Harry received his largest order yet for parachutes. He asked the girls to all work overlapping ten hour shifts. He brought in more sewing machines borrowed from neighbouring Stretford. Even the backroom was emptied to accommodate an additional six machines. The three shifts continued with each person overlapping four hours into the next shift. One evening while Kay, Veronica, Constance, and Hilda worked, an air raid sounded. It was no different than any other. The girls hid themselves below their machines.

Kay's work space was located beside Constance's. She could hear her wince with pain next to her. At first she wasn't sure but amid the sounds of the sirens and bombers flying overhead a faint whimpering could be heard.

Kay crawled over to her. Constance lay curled up, holding her abdomen.

"What is wrong?"

"I think it's the baby. I think I ruptured my water."

Constance looked frightened and was obviously in a terrible amount of discomfort.

"I'll get Hilda. She'll know what to do."

Kay crawled to Hilda. Her first child had been born just after the start of the war. She was the only woman in the room who'd experienced childbirth aside from Edith's mother Bette whose workstation was clear across the room.

"What are you doing? Are you daft girl?"

"It's Constance. Her water's ruptured- she thinks."

Hilda made the sign of the cross and told Kay to go to the back, fetch whatever scraps of material she could find.

"What about the baby?"

"It's too soon for the baby. She is only a little over five months. Now, go get what I asked of you."

Kay ran to the backroom. An incendiary bomb landed somewhere nearby and the floor shook knocking her to the ground. She crawled the remaining distance and grabbed what scraps she could find in the dim room. She slowly made her way back to Constance and Hilda. There was a pool of water around Constance on the floor and Kay knew enough about the birthing process to know this wasn't a good sign this early in pregnancy. Hilda was correct- five months was too soon for the baby to be born. Kay must turn her attention to Constance and hope for the best.

Constance was sweating profusely and looked grave.

"You must be brave, child." Hilda placed her hand on Constance's abdomen. "You're having contractions and your water's broken. This means the baby is coming- early. Very early."

"I don't want to lose my baby." Constance cried.

"I know, my dear, but sometimes these things are beyond our control."

Constance screamed out in pain.

Kay looked over at Veronica and Theresa who both crept from their workstations, braving the bombing to see what all the commotion was. Kay shook her head at both of them encouraging them to stay where they were. Harry came crawling over and a knowing look crossed his face. Not wanting to mortify Constance, he went back behind the till to ride out the air raid.

The delivery was of a fast and awful sort. The contractions came swiftly one after another and eventually with them came an awful bloody mess. There was so much blood Kay was sure it couldn't possibly be normal. Hilda worked feverishly to stem the blood flow, packing Constance with folded pieces of cloth Kay cut for her at regular intervals. After thirty minutes of intense, gruelling work, Constance lay nearly passed out, with Kay and Hilda spent.

"The bleeding's stopped. We need to get her to the hospital."

Hilda called to Harry who came with a large cloth and called all of the girls over.

"If we lay her on this ladies, I'll get the end with her head. Kay and Veronica on one side. Hilda and Theresa on the other. The hospital is several blocks away but if we work together we can make it."

There was a lull in the bombing and the other women peered out from under their work stations. Bette was among them and volunteered to hold the blanket at the area near Constance's feet. She and Hilda shared knowing looks. The blanket served as a makeshift gurney and within minutes they were on their way to the hospital. The street outside was littered with debris. The area surrounding the sewing shop had taken a direct hit. It was a wonder their shop was still standing. People emerged from the smoky, bombed out buildings searching for survivors- each one too caught up in his or her own search to assist in their tragedy.

Constance now slipped into a coma-like sleep. Kay hoped it was just that, a sleep. She could see her chest still rising and falling. The group of women, guided by Harry, made their way through the streets of Manchester towards the hospital. Fifteen minutes later they were securely inside and met with a nurse who helped them lay her on a bed. Hilda explained what transpired.

The nurse asked after her husband. Kay quickly interjected. She advised the nurse of how he was off at war, but her parents would be notified straight away. Kay knew in her heart that lying about a husband and his whereabouts was wrong but couldn't bring herself to tell the truth. There was no reason to add to Constance's embarrassment. Kay turned and fled the hospital. She hated leaving Constance but knew she would be in good hands with Hilda. Hilda asked the nurse to fetch her own husband who was a doctor.

Outside Kay wiped her blood covered hands on her skirt and walked as quickly as she could to Constance's home. She found her elderly parents at home and told them of the news. Her father appeared like he may collapse right then and there. Kay offered to stay with him while a neighbour, Angela, escorted her mother to the hospital.

Kay sat up for hours waiting for an update. Constance's father fell asleep in his chair and Kay covered his feet and legs with a blanket. It wasn't until the following morning when Anthony finally came with news.

It was just as Kay expected. Constance would make it, but the baby hadn't. Anthony and Kay walked home, arm in arm.

"She's doing all right considering."

Anthony had gone to the shop and Harry told him where Edith and her mum were. He'd headed straight to the hospital where Veronica and Theresa were keeping watch until Constance's mother arrived.

"Are you going up to the hospital?"

"Yes. I will go see her this afternoon." Kay mumbled.

"Maybe take her some flowers from the garden."

"I will."

Kay wasn't sure what she was feeling in this moment. Sadness and grief- a hint of relief. Constance had been excited about the baby regardless of the circumstances, but in the end it hadn't been up to her. The stress of the war had proven too much. It had taken its toll on another innocent victim.

Kay went upstairs and stripped down to bathe. Her hands were washed but the rest of her bore the stench of blood. She put her skirt in the bin, not wanting to wear it or remember the events of yesterday ever again. She laid in the hot water, which due to water restrictions came only to mid-thigh. Over an hour later the last of the warmth crept out of it and a chill began to invade her bones. She climbed out and piled her hair high on her head. She donned a pretty dress and some sensible shoes. She sat on the edge of the bed and sobbed. The next thing she knew she was being gently coaxed awake by Ray.

He held her for long moments rubbing her back.

"I know all about Constance . Anthony told me downstairs. If you sleep much longer you'll miss seeing her at the hospital. Come on. I'll walk you."

Hand in hand they walked to the hospital. Outside the streets of Manchester were bustling with activity. It was strange the way disaster struck day after day- night after night. Tragedy and loss surrounded them. Then as if nothing happened, citizens would pick up right where they'd left off and continue on. Most days that's what Kay did as well but she felt Constance's loss as deeply as if it had been her own.

At the hospital she was reluctant to walk inside Constance's room. She wasn't sure how to hide her feelings of sadness. Furthermore she wasn't sure if male visitors would be welcome. As if Ray read her thoughts, he politely offered to wait outside. Kay walked in and had to do a double take at the sight of Harry at Constance's bedside. He held a gorgeous nosegay of daffodils, a box of chocolates, and a meat pie in his lap.

It was the first time Kay saw Harry as something other than their boss. He was a man like any other. A very nice looking man. If she had to guess, she would still guess him to be in his late thirties- not nearly as old as the other girls had previously argued and certainly not as old as any of their fathers. His hair was black without any hint of grey and his eyes were blue. He could be described as having very refined good looks. As far as she knew, he hadn't dated since moving to Manchester just before the war. From the looks of it, his concern for Constance exceeded that of the concern a mere boss might have for his employee.

He stood and excused himself when Kay arrived, smiling at her scrutiny of his looks and presence. He walked out the door merely nodding to her as he passed. When she was sure he was out of earshot, Constance spoke.

"Don't say it. I can see it written all over your face."

Even in light of the situation, she was as feisty as ever.

"I wasn't going to say a thing. How are you feeling, my friend?"

"I am better than I felt yesterday. It was awful, Kay, but I will get past it."

"You will. You're strong, Constance. Strong enough for all of us."

Kay reached out and held her hand squeezing it lightly.

"Thank you for getting my mum. When I opened my eyes and she was here it was just what I needed to see. I thought they'd have been so angry with me about the baby- but they weren't. Not really. They were so supportive from the beginning. Even now, she reassured me my day to have a child will come. Some day. In God's time."

"It will, as will all of ours. This war was too much. It would've been for any woman." Kay paused. "Is there anything you need?"

"Nothing."

Her eyes closed a bit and Kay could tell she was weak and tired.

"Good. Ray is waiting outside and I don't want to keep him. I'll see you soon."

"I don't plan on being in here too long. Keep sending the G.I.'s notes for me."

"I will."

Kay was glad to see the bad experiences with one G.I. hadn't soured Constance to the whole lot of them. Most of them were wonderful men, she just happened to hook up with the one who had been deceitful. The whole idea of it made Kay feel sick to her stomach. In time Constance would meet someone and fall in love again. She'd move past the horrible wounds and scars caused by this war. Her time for happiness would come- Kay just knew it.

Ray waited outside in the garden smoking a cigarette.

"How is she?"

"Better than expected."

"I saw Harry stopped by. He's a nice man."

"Yes, I know. He's a bit older than her though."

"Not much. You never know."

Ray took Kay to the railway station.

"Where are we going?"

"I thought I'd surprise you. We're taking a trip to Stanley Park in Blackpool."

"It's been so long since I've seen the lake. I can imagine how beautiful it will be this time of year. The flowers in bloom, the ducks, and swans."

A short time later they were lounging on a blanket in the park. The summer sun warmed everything around them. The sweet smell of jasmine and lilac on the breeze. Kay lay with her head in Ray's lap.

"Ray, I've received a letter from Jon and one from George as well. I'd written them about our wedding plans and the fact we'd move to the States afterwards. Though I'd discussed the possibility of it all with them before- it seems they've reconsidered and now think it's a horrible idea."

"They're not happy about it."

"No, they're not. Both feel it is silly for me to have become involved with a foreigner. Their letters are harsh but only out of concern. They were fine with us dating- and even getting married. It seems they thought we'd reconsider the move and remain here. They see the move as splitting up the family."

"Are you having second thoughts?"

"No, I just hope in time they'll understand and be more accepting."

A single tear rolled down her cheek. Ray lifted his hand to wipe it away.

"What of Anthony and Billy?"

"Anthony loves you and Billy knew of you through Jimmy's letters. That won his approval long ago. It's just George and Jonathan are my oldest brothers- sort of father figures to me. I want their blessing, too."

"Well, there is still time."

"I'd like for them all to be here for it."

"I don't know if it's possible."

"We could wait until after the war to get married."

"We could but then I'll be demobilised. We run the risk I'll be shipped out before our wedding date, but if waiting is what you want to do- we'll wait."

Kay hugged Ray and led him to the water's edge.

"Anyone ever swim here?"

"Not really. It may be June but the water is still chilly."

"Looks fine to me."

Ray swept Kay up into his arms and carried her into the lake squealing.

"Ray! I have nothing dry to change into!"

"I'll buy you a frock in one of the shops."

Kay voiced no other complaints. They enjoyed a beautiful day of swimming and sunbathing. Later they shared a picnic dinner followed by some shopping. They stayed the night with some friends of Ray's- an American G.I. named Joe that was married to a British girl from Blackpool.

Joe's wife Mary still lived at home with her parents. Joe would visit on leave. They had plans to return to the United States after the war and make a life there together. Mary and Kay sat talking about the war and how they wished it would end. Mary and Joe were expecting their first baby, and she was due in late February. She was so excited about the baby, as were her parents.

The recent loss of Constance's baby colored Kay's view of having children during the war. Kay was terrified of the prospect of it. She couldn't imagine finding herself in a similar position and was glad for her it wasn't a possibility. Of course she didn't say as much.

It turns out Joe was from Boston, Mass. He and Ray were close friends, having met during the war. Kay didn't know much about the United States, but to hear Mary tell it they'd be neighbours. The distance between Boston and North Brookfield wasn't much. Kay felt an immediate sense of relief in knowing at least one person when she arrived in the USA. Joe was a pilot and upon his return would go back to work at the airport. His job awaited him. He owned his own home and it seemed as if he and Mary had it all sussed out. It was in this moment Kay realised she knew very little about Ray, his family, and what their future would hold. It frightened her. Maybe her brothers were right. Where did he work? Did he own a house? Where would they live exactly?

Kay thought it over and decided these were all questions she might want answered. Was he able to provide for a wife and family? Kay heard him speak of his brothers and one sister. Their family owned an airfield and aeroplane shop. Besides that she was clueless. She loved him. She wanted to marry him. In the end did anything else matter?

Even if she married a British man nothing would be certain. Of course her family was here- or would be after the war. In America she'd have only the family of her husband…and her newly found friend, Mary. Beyond that she'd have no one. Would she be lonely? These thoughts plagued her throughout the night as she tried to sleep in the guest room. She stared at the ceiling and tried to imagine a life with Ray…a life far, far away.

She had seen pictures of the United States in books. Large open expanses of land, quaint farms and small towns. They certainly had more industry and probably good shopping. Kay knew a combination of fear and nerves were driving her imagination beyond what was sensible. She decided to make herself go to sleep. Will herself to sleep. At dawn Ray knocked on her door and told her to get dressed. They needed to catch a train back to Manchester and then he must be on his way to Warrington. Before they left for the depot a post office telegram arrived addressed to Mrs. Joe Renault. Mary opened it and read silently. She looked up, her eyes filled with a mixture of fear and hope. She handed the telegram to Kay who read it aloud.

INVASION NORMUNDY HAS BEGUN. WEEKEND HOME CANCELLED. JOE

"It's happening. The Allied invasion in France."

Kay embraced Mary.

"I'll pray for Joe's safety." Kay offered.

"I must return to the base. Will you be all right to return to Manchester alone?" Ray asked.

"I'll be fine."

An hour later Kay felt tired. The gentle rocking of the train lulled her. She was too tired to worry about it further. She wondered about her brothers. The way Mary explained it this would be an enormous operation. The train passengers were abuzz with the news of the Allied invasion. It was an all-out air and water attack. Kay's mind drifted to Anthony, Billy, George and Jonathan. Had any of them been brought over for the attack?

Young Anthony had only just joined the Navy, and was deployed earlier this month. He'd finally turned nineteen and his time had come. Jon was so far away- she doubted he was there. Billy and George were very likely involved. Then there was Ray. She hoped he would remain safely on the base, but she had her doubts. He was a pilot. He'd flown many missions, he'd likely fly many more. Kay realised their lives were closely intertwined- forever. The thought of losing him was more than she could stand. Her mind was made up. She'd marry Ray at the end of the war. She'd follow him anywhere. They'd make a life together. It would be a good one. All of her previous worries were nonsense. She pushed them aside and looked forward.

The assault at Normandy went on and on. For days the women clung to the wireless radio, their only lifeline to the men they loved. By early July they began to wonder if the invasion at Normandy would ever cease. Thousands had died as death reports came flooding in. Friends, neighbours and even one of Edith's brothers- lost their lives. As quickly as the forces ran ashore they were mowed down. Kay could only wonder at the hell they were living.

In between radio broadcasts the women continued to sew. It was all there was to busy their minds and hearts. Every time a telegram arrived, all of the women cringed, praying it wasn't addressed to them. When one arrived addressed to Kay her heart froze in her chest. She took it from the courier and walked back over to her machine to open it.

ALL IS WELL. RAY

While relieved at this news, she still knew nothing of her brothers. By mid-July the success of the D-day Invasion spread throughout England. The allied forces successfully claimed five beaches and pushed inland to establish landing zones needed for reinforcements. From that moment forward there was a marked turning point in the war. Everyone was elated at the knowledge that the end of this chaotic struggle was just around the corner. Ray's visits stopped altogether and she had no hopes of seeing him again anytime soon. Even more worrisome was the fact that Kay still hadn't received word from any of her brothers as weeks passed and became months.

She and Theresa fretted, doing the best they could just to keep busy. No one wanted to be alone. The women banded together finding solace in friendship. Theresa feared for George but still kept hope. Young Edith kept her worries about Anthony to herself. They wrote letters and kept right on mailing them to the last known addresses they had for each. Kay wrote to Jonathan and Billy, knowing neither had a wife nor a girlfriend to write to them. The days of winter came and supplies grew more scarce.

By the end of March, Kay received a letter from Mary.

Dear Kay,

I hope this letter finds you in good health and with happy news of your brothers and Ray. Molly was born in late February. She is a healthy, fine baby. Joe has been stationed in Germany these last months. He is well. While the winter has been cold, he said they're having much success and he hopes the war will be over soon.

Once demobilisation begins it will be swift. I am writing to let you know I've made application in London for my passport. Other war brides are doing the same, following the same process. I don't know how this will differ for you as you're not married yet.

There are many brides and the travel details aren't known at this time. That being said I'm excited about the journey no matter when it may come. Let's pray this war ends soon. Take care and God bless. Mary

Kay was shocked to hear her speaking of demobilisation. She sure hoped Mary was right...the war was going to end quickly. The weeks continued to crawl past with no further word from Ray. Edith received a letter from Anthony. He was safe and sound. He'd been off the southern coast of England at the time of the invasion. His letter talked of hope of a German surrender. When Edith read his letter aloud the entire sewing shop went up in a cheer.

Then a few weeks later news came. A radio broadcast announced the end of the war. Harry brought out a bottle of Cognac he kept hidden in the back room and opened it to share with all. That day marked the end of the sewing of parachutes. The end of sadness and the beginning of a new life. Harry announced the closing of the shop for a few weeks simply stating he needed some time off. No one complained.

Everyone ran into the streets. There was dancing, singing, and drinking. Kay ran to her house and helped everyone pack their things. All of her housemates were heading home in anticipation of the men's return. Edith left her address and contact information for Anthony and asked Kay to give them to him when he returned home. While the goodbyes were tearful, they were joyous as well. A few days later Kay received a brief telegram from Ray letting her know he was alive and well.

Then he surprised Kay by coming to visit her in early September. She wasn't expecting him. He looked tired and dishevelled, but very happy.

"I brought you something."

He produced a tin cup containing two eggs. It had been so long since she'd seen an egg. She was elated.

"Where'd you get them?"

"I passed a farmer on my way to the station selling eggs. You've mentioned not being able to get them, so I figured I'd trade him for a few. Thought you might want to bake a cake."

"I certainly would. What did you trade with him for?"

"A pack of cigarettes."

"I think you got the better end of the bargain."

Kay walked into the kitchen and set out flour, shortening, and the eggs.

"I received a letter from Mary, Joe's wife. It turns out she has put in for her passport. I guess the demobilisation of American troops will begin shortly. Unfortunately I've received no word about the British troops. I don't know when my brothers will be home."

"That's the reason for my visit. My demobilisation may happen as early as the end of this year."

"The end of this year? That is fast."

Ray came over to stand in front of her.

"Charlie, I know we wanted to wait for your brothers' return but if we do I may not be here for our wedding. I think we may need to seriously discuss setting a wedding date in the near future."

"I see." Kay said. She set the mixing bowl and wooden spoon down on the counter in front of her. "I agree with you. Maybe if I send a note to each of them they'll be able to attend."

"What do you think about October 30th? I've checked and there shouldn't be any problem with my leave getting approved for that time."

"An autumn wedding sounds perfect. I have to put the finishing touches on my dress. I'm not sure a little over a month will be sufficient enough time for me to finish it."

"My parents wanted to attend our wedding. If you aren't able to finish it bring it home with you. We can have a second ceremony there." Seeing the disappointment on Kay's face Ray gently held both of her elbows and spoke into her eyes. "The important thing is we are married before I leave. They won't let you come to the States without us being husband and wife. We'll get married here in front of family and friends. It's what really matters."

"You're right. You'll make the arrangements for my passage?"

"Yes."

"I think the most important thing to me is we're married in the church in front of God. We'll have to go together to amend the bands with the church today. I'd still like to get married at the Church of the Holy Name on Oxford Road in Manchester. I like Father Brennon there and have attended there for years."

"Perfect. I will write to each of your brothers myself, explaining to them my intentions, so they hear it firsthand."

"Thank you. It would mean a lot to me."

Kay stood sifting flour. She knew Ray was correct- there was no time to lose. The war was over. He could be demobilised anytime now. If they waited she may find herself without a groom. Her brothers would understand the circumstances she found herself in. They'd have to.

The following week she received word from Jonathan he'd be home first on the fifteenth of September, followed by Billy on the seventh of October and George on the twelfth. It seemed only Anthony would miss her wedding. He sent a lovely card with a small pearl bracelet in it he purchased in France. She went to her room and ran her hands over her half finished wedding gown. She'd worked feverishly on it for days and still it wouldn't be completed in time for the church ceremony. Yet, there was always hope of it being completed later. An American wedding where they renewed their vows could be wonderful. At the end of the day, whether she wore it here or there wouldn't be important. The fact they were married, husband and wife, until death do them part was all that truly mattered. They'd survived the war, loss and sadness to go forward and live a new life.

Chapter Twelve

The smell of saltwater and fish flooded Christine's nostrils the following afternoon as they strolled along a beach. The aroma and slight breeze were pleasant. Everything was just as her grandmother described it. Morecambe Bay had been the location of her and Grandpa's honeymoon so long ago. Now Christine would get to experience it for herself. Gulls soared overhead. An enormous pier jetted out into the surf where a restaurant sat perched on it located near the end. Fishermen dotted the pier's expanse, fishing from its edges. It was low tide and in the sand there were boats and old ships. Each one buried up to its hull or higher in the sand.

Christine had visions of horrific storms- the kinds of legend. Seafarers washed ashore and slammed into rocks on the coastline. The only problem with her imaginary tales was there weren't any rocks in sight. What could have caused these boats to get grounded like this?

"What happened to those, Grandma?"

"You probably didn't notice the signs but it is quicksand."

"Quicksand?"

"Yes- of sorts. They warn people to stay out of the sand. If the boats come too close to shoreline, after the tide goes out they'll become trapped in the sand. As you can see most of them don't get out of it."

Her grandmother laughed and her eyes danced in the sunlight.

"When your grandfather and I visited here I knew about the sand of Morecambe Bay, but being a Yank he didn't. So there he is walking closer and closer to the deep sand at low tide. I stayed way up on firm ground watching him venture down into the sand to collect sea shells and such. I wondered how far to let him go. You see there weren't any signs then to warn you of the danger. Finally a man yells from the shoreline 'Hey you crazy Yank! Can't you see that's bloody quicksand? Get out of there!' Your grandpa sprinted out of there so fast. He never let me live it down. He claimed he'd survived the war only to nearly die entrapped by quicksand."

"You were a mischievous one."

"I was. He'd had so much fun at my expense from time to time- I figured why not have a little fun at his. Oh- I wouldn't have let him drown. He'd have figured out it was quicksand long before that happened."

"It's kind of eerie with all of the trapped boats."

"Pretty neat, huh? At high tide they look like shipwrecks. The first time I saw them even I didn't know the reason they were here."

Christine glanced at the shops lining the bay shore.

"Those weren't here then. It's become quite touristy compared to how it used to be. If you're game there's somewhere I'd like to go. We can take a cab but after we get there it'll require a short walk."

"Of course. Let's grab Mom. I think she's in the shop over there."

Moments later they were in a cab heading north into the countryside- away from the sea. The landscape became more hilly and sheep grazed in pastures. Wild ivy grew on the fences trellising along the roadside. They came to a small bridge where it crossed a canal with a set of lochs and what appeared to be a mill to their left. Her grandmother asked the cab driver to stop there.

"We'll get out here."

Connie paid the driver and they all climbed out.

"Where are we going, Grandma?"

"First things first- we're going to grab a pint."

Christine glanced around. To her left there was a long winding gravel road with a mill in the distance, and more sheep. To her front there was a country road which continued northwest and then disappeared in the distance. Behind her was the road returning to the town of Morecambe, quite a distance away. To her right, down a small lane a short distance was an old inn, two stories in height with a stone foundation, an elevated stoop, and one outside lamp lit. It appeared dank and dark- not exactly the kind of place she'd choose to have a pint.

"In there?" Christine questioned.

"Yes."

Her grandmother led the way down the quiet lane towards the inn. They climbed the steps one at a time. It was beginning to mist and the steps were covered in a green algae which was becoming slippery. When they opened the door all eyes were on them. There were a dozen or so people inside- all downing a beer. Two large yellow labs lifted their heads from their slumber in acknowledgement of the strangers but made no move to come over and greet them. After they decided they weren't anyone of consequence the dogs laid their heads back down and resumed their snooze.

"Seat yourselves." A woman called from behind the bar.

Everyone did as she asked and moments later she came to take their order. Christine glanced out the window next to their table and found it was beginning to rain even harder.

"Supposed to blow a gale today."

"Blow a gale?" Christine asked.

"Storm Dear." Her grandmother explained. Next she ordered several orders of fish and chips along with pints all around. The waitress disappeared.

"What is this place, Grandma?"

"I came here once with your Grandfather on our honeymoon. He was a sucker for rides in the country. Of course we are still very close to the sea."

Christine thought back to the story her grandmother shared with her as a small child about the quaint English inn in the countryside where she'd spent two days on her honeymoon. This wasn't exactly what she'd envisioned.

"How do you know we are still close to the sea?"

"The lochs- the canals you saw outside." Her mother clarified.

"Oh. Cool."

"Your Grandfather had never been here and in this particular area- when you're out you're out and when you're in- you're in." Her grandmother smiled and winked at her.

"What does that mean?"

"When the tide comes in it surrounds everything. If you're on this side of the road when it comes in it surrounds everything- the homes- the shops- everything."

"What about the roads?"

"They'll be covered until the tide goes back out."

"Underwater?" She shrieked.

Christine jumped up and ran over to the front door. She opened it and peered outside. Sure enough- what Grandma said was true. The tide was coming in. The water was already creeping its way around the inn and up towards the front door. Christine rushed back over to the table.

"Holy cow! Its the coolest thing ever, Grandma- but don't you think we should get out of here?" She would never confess to feeling a little uneasy. At least it was just until the tide went back out- however long that would be.

"No. Just the opposite. I think we should stay the night. The weather's turned nasty outside and there is still somewhere special I want to go. We can go tomorrow. I remember being here on my honeymoon- trapped inside our room for hours at a time while the tide was in. It was quite romantic really."

Christine couldn't help but feel this was a terrible idea but before she could object her mom was agreeing with her grandmother. She in no way wanted to be a party pooper but she had to admit to being nervous about staying the night in the run down inn, during a gale no less- and trapped by the sea. This was certainly not her idea of a relaxing stay in the countryside.

"Let's get Christine another beer. She looks scared." Her mother teased.

"I am scared." Christine lowered her voice to a whisper. "This place is scaring me."

"I saw a sign saying tonight is karaoke night." Her mom grinned from across the table.

"Hurray!" Christine squealed sarcastically.

Christine downed three more beers and found her trepidation blowing away with the wind outside. Suffice to say, with the bad weather and all, the karaoke crowd was sparse. A few hours later she found herself belting out a horrible rendition of *Stand by Your Man* with an Englishman old enough to be her father. Grandma dazzled every one present with *The White Cliffs of Dover*. By the time they turned in well after midnight Christine decided this inn could be better described as magical rather than the scary experience she first thought it would turn out to be.

When the sun rose early the next morning, Grandma was already dressed and ready for breakfast. Christine was a little more lethargic due largely in part to the multiple pints of ale she'd downed. Wanting nothing more than to cover her head with the bed pillow, she instead opted to drag herself out of bed and go in search of coffee.

"Dress warmly."

"I only have the one outfit- my options are limited."

"I had a feeling your grandma would want to stay so I packed a few things in my backpack. I laid a sweater out on the chair for you as well as some leggings. I'll see you at breakfast. Don't worry I'll have a cup of strong tea waiting for you."

"Coffee if they have it."

How ridiculous is this? I got outdrank by my eighty year old grandmother and mom?

Christine stumbled downstairs ten minutes later to find her grandmother and mother in good spirits chatting away with a local woman who'd apparently offered to run them to Thurnham Hall- wherever that was.

Christine sipped her tea, bummed they didn't have any coffee- and took a few nibbles of her scone deciding too much too soon would be a bad idea with her stomach turning flips as it was.

Grandma ate like a trucker, putting away two pieces of toast, some Canadian bacon, and even found room for a scone with butter and jam. Her mother was no slouch either. What was wrong with her?

Thirty minutes later the jostling of the backseat of the small car proved to be too much for her stomach. While she didn't get sick she knew she would if she didn't get out of the car soon. She was glad when the woman who could've doubled as an Indy car driver, came to a halt at the end of a long driveway. Her mother thanked her and they began their walk towards the enormous building which must have been Thurnam Hall in the distance. The cool wind blowing on her face and neck quickly revived Christine and she knew she'd survive the day.

Hereford cows grazed in the fields surrounding them. The grass was still wet with dewdrops and the roadway splattered with mud from yesterday's rain. It was cooler than it had been in Manchester or Wigan. The change in weather was refreshing and while others complained about the wet weather Christine must admit to enjoying it immensely.

"Your grandfather and I picnicked here during our honeymoon- it was just as lovely then as it is today. There were sheep where the cattle are today. Behind the hall there is a gorgeous duck pond filled with ducks, geese and swans- of course we've just missed the swan upping. Christine would've enjoyed that."

"The swan upping?"

"All swans are the property of the Queen and must be accounted for. So each year there is a swan upping where they are tagged."

"I think I would've enjoyed at least trying it." Christine surprised even herself with the notion that 'upping' and tagging any sort of animal could actually have been fun.

Thurnham Hall appeared to be three stories in height. It was a large stone building reminiscent of a small scale castle. At one end there was a small chapel and at its centre there were doors leading into the Great Hall. Christine felt it was small in comparison to Glamis, but upon entering its front doors she realised how large it really was. While it was nowhere on the same scale as a Glamis Castle or Windsor, it was large even in comparison to the mansions in the States.

They walked into the hall and were greeted by an enormous room filled with a few people. A large Tudor fireplace contained a small fire burning brightly within. Christine went to warm her hands in front of it. Her grandmother sat down on an oversized leather sofa accompanied by her mother. A waitress appeared to take their order offering them tea, brandy, or even Scotch. Christine refused the alcoholic beverages and instead asked for a soda. After the waitress walked away, the front door opened and a woman entered the hall. She waved to her grandmother and slowly walked across the room to greet them.

Her grandmother stood and introduced her as Constance. Christine immediately recognised the name and rose to shake her hand. Constance was a strikingly beautiful woman who must have been even more gorgeous in her youth. She took a seat with Kay and Connie on the couch. Within moments the two older women were reminiscing. Christine and her mother excused themselves to walk around the back of the castle and visit with the ducks and geese outside. There were more people visiting than she first thought. At least half a dozen walked around the small pond fishing or just enjoying the cool day. Christine made conversation with a few of the older gentlemen inquiring as to how many fish they'd caught this morning. After a short conversation with a man named Alfred they continued towards the back of the pond where a stone wall outlined the perimeter in the distance.

There was a small building at the back of the property which housed an indoor workout centre, pool and spa. Connie inquired about manicures for the three of them and was disappointed to learn there weren't any appointments available for the remainder of the day. There were openings for tomorrow but she knew they wouldn't be an option. They'd be back in Wigan by that time. They exited the building and continued back to the main hall. Christine put Thurnham Hall on her list of places to return and visit someday. She thought the fishing might be something Jeff would enjoy, maybe even something they could do together. She wasn't sure how he'd feel about a few spa treatments but it couldn't hurt to ask.

Inside her grandmother sat visiting with the stunning older woman. Constance appeared to be in her mid-eighties. Her silver streaked hair was pulled high on her head revealing high cheekbones and bright green eyes. She sat, shoulders back, filled with poise and confidence. Her voice was even and possessed an overall calming effect. She was warm and friendly. She spoke addressing her question to Christine.

"So, I hear you're engaged?"

"I am. We're getting married in March."

"A spring wedding. I had a spring wedding myself. I'll bet Florida in the spring is quite lovely."

"We get a bit of rain but overall it is usually much milder than summer. Summertime in Florida is really hot and muggy. My wedding is going to be held inside though- and in the evening."

"Sounds wonderful. Tell me about your young man."

Christine wasn't sure what she wanted to know so she just started at the beginning. She told her how they'd met at Professor Archambeau's office four years earlier. He'd won her over with his slight accent and wavy black hair. His eyes were sea foam green and his skin tanned. He was much taller than Christine herself, standing at just over six feet tall. He possessed the fit build of an athlete but wasn't overly muscled.

He was a quiet romantic. He enjoyed fine wines and outings to a local vineyard to listen to live music on weekends. Picnicking at the beach was one of their favourite things to do. The more Christine talked about him the more she realised her reasons for falling in love with him in the first place. He made her happy. He was seldom moody or angry. He made her feel like the most beautiful woman alive.

She shared with Constance his penchant for gift giving- whatever the occasion. A muffler for her trip to England was just one of many thoughtful things he did through the years. She related to them how on one occasion he sent her roses on a Thursday just because he loved her. Sure they disagreed from time to time. Their recent argument over the wedding menu and type of cake which would be served would surely be the first among many squabbles.

"It sounds like your Jeffrey is a good fellow. A man who likes to treat his wife with kindness and generosity is hard to find. It took me a while to appreciate those qualities in my own husband, but I eventually became wise and married him."

Constance shared the tale about her engagement and subsequent marriage. Christine knew from her grandmother's accounts of the war about Constance's love and loss with an American G.I. It warmed her heart to know this woman had gone on to find true love and happiness.

Chapter Thirteen

November 1945

Manchester, England

Kay sat quietly knitting a small baby jumper in yellow. She wasn't expecting but knew Ray was right- after getting married it would be a real possibility. A light rap came at the window of her back door. She stood to answer it. Constance came waltzing in, as if floating on air. She beamed at Kay. Kay looked her over and stopped short at the appearance of a ruby on her left ring finger.

"Does the ruby ring mean what I think it means?"

"It does. Harry asked me to marry him last night and I

accepted."

"I didn't realise things had gotten so serious between you two."

Constance took a seat in the living room. Kay came to sit beside her.

"It just sort of happened. When he closed the shop a few months ago after the war he just sort of popped up at my door. He visited with my parents. The next thing I knew he was a regular stopping by for tea a few times every week."

"Go on."

"Then, after your wedding he started hinting around at wanting to settle down himself. We had a few conversations about family, life and marriage. At this point our teas became more like dates with me walking him out and him stealing a kiss or two. I knew he liked me. He is rather attractive- don't you think?"

"I do."

"And you don't think he is too old for me?"

"My parents had fifteen years between them. It didn't seem to matter." Kay confided.

"I agree. So I said yes- obviously. Have you received Ray's

demobilisation orders?"

"Not yet."

"I want you to be there. I'd like to have it in the spring when the roses are in bloom."

"I think that's a wonderful idea. What about the dress?"

"I've just begun making it. Harry said I could open a dress shop!"

"It sounds marvellous."

"Would you like to come work with me until you leave for the United States?"

"That would be grand."

In an instant, realization crossed Kay's mind. The war was finished. Troops were being demobilised. They had gotten married in October as planned. Now it was November and Ray's orders would surely come soon. She'd be leaving her family, her friends, and even her home to go to America. It was just around the corner-possibly only weeks away. She was suddenly frightened. She thought she was prepared for this, but maybe she wasn't.

All of her brothers were home now. Anthony the last to arrive only just last week. He'd immediately sought out Edith and proposed. She'd gladly accepted. They were set to wed the following summer. Jonathan was scheduled to return to Scotland by mid-February where his bride awaited him. They'd live in Stirling. George and Theresa would stay right here in Manchester to be near to her family. Billy would stay as well. He'd just started seeing a nice girl uptown, but wasn't looking to get married anytime soon.

Kay pondered the situation further. All of her brothers would remain in Europe, even Scotland wasn't too far away, a short half-day trip by rail. He could be home for holidays and visit whenever he wished…really. Kay was going to America. All the way across the ocean- by ship. Later the same afternoon the postman came with another letter from Mary which only heightened the tension Kay already felt.

Dear Kay,

I've just received word of Joe's demobilisation. It is scheduled for February. My passport was issued and arrived this last week. Molly will be nearly one year by that time. I'm waiting for my travel itinerary and hope I will not be so very far behind Joe in my arrival to the States. He is excited for us to meet his family and be joined on a more permanent basis. His mother and sisters wrote me last week welcoming me into the family.

I hope all is well. I will write again soon when I know more.
God bless. Mary

Kay sat in silence holding the opened letter. She knew she should feel the way Mary felt. Elated, overjoyed even. The unfortunate acknowledgement of her anxiety filled feelings was disheartening. Her heart hurt at the thought of leaving. Leaving behind her brothers and the only home she'd ever known- Jolly Old England.

Boots came to climb into her lap. She petted his black fur lovingly.

"I can't imagine it. I don't want to leave you behind, Boots, but I must. Anthony and Edith will take good care of you, I know it."

For days Kay worked to push her feelings to the back of her mind. She continued making all of the necessary arrangements to leave. She'd filed her passport documents the Monday following her wedding. She knew her request was being processed. She made a trip to the market and returned with groceries to find she'd received a telegram.

During the war she'd been apprehensive about telegrams out

of fear of losing one of her brothers or Ray. Today's apprehension stemmed from an entirely different place. Billy handed it to her when she came in the front door. Kay just set it aside on the table and began unpacking her bag of groceries.

"Aren't you going to open it, Katie?"

"I wasn't planning on it. Not just yet."

"It's from, Ray."

"I know. I saw."

"Are you all right- the two of you?"

"We are."

"Then, what's bothering you?"

"Nothing in particular."

"If you're not going to open it then I will."

"Suit yourself."

While Kay didn't want to open the telegram herself, she decided allowing her brother to open it may actually be easier on her nerves. She put the kettle on and waited for him to read it, but instead he handed it to her- opened.

"You're a married woman now. Read it." He slid his chair in and left the kitchen.

DEMOB TUESDAY, FEBRUARY 12TH ARRIVE HOME STATES FEBRUARY 26TH, I APPLIED FOR YOUR PASSAGE=RAY

Kay moped around for the remainder of the afternoon. The weather was dreary and a slow drizzling rain set in. She knew what she must do and resolved to do so first thing in the morning. She climbed the stairs to her room and pulled the covers high over her head and cried long and hard.

A few hours later Constance stood at her door.

"May I come in?"

When Kay merely nodded she came in and sat at the foot of the bed.

"Jonathan called me a while ago. He's worried about you."

"I don't see why. It's not his concern."

"I saw Ray's demobilisation information downstairs."

"I'm not going."

"You're not going! How can you say such things?"

Kay made no attempt to answer.

"You don't need me to tell you- I think you know. You're a married woman, Kay. Married. That is that."

"I don't see how it matters."

"Well of course it matters. What about Ray? Don't you love him?"

"Of course, I love him!" Kay sobbed into her pillow.

"Then, the answer is clear. You must have known this war would end! You must have known this when you accepted his hand and became his wife- eventually you'd have to go with him! This couldn't all come as a surprise!"

Kay remained face down in the pillow. Constance laid her hand on her calf and lowered her voice to a mere whisper.

"I know it's scary. We've all had to face scary things, but you should look on this as an adventure. Do you know how many women would love to take your place? To be married to a wonderful G.I. and have this amazing opportunity to go to the states?"

"Let them have it! Let them go! I'm staying here."

"I'm ashamed of you, Kay. Ashamed. You're a lady and no less. Your integrity and manners don't allow for such behaviour. In the end you will do the right and sensible thing. Your honour and love for Ray demands no less."

Constance stood to go. Kay made no attempt to stop her. She

lay in bed crying until early the next morning. When she finally appeared in the kitchen just after dawn, her brothers Jonathan and Billy sat drinking coffee. Both stood when she entered and offered her his seat. Neither of them brought up the telegram or asked about her feelings on the subject. In her heart she knew they considered it a done deal. She knew it was as well. Her reluctance to leave her family and home were only that. There was no use in speaking about something which would only upset them all.

They both hugged her goodbye and headed out to work. Kay decided to catch a bus to Harry's to mend things with Constance. When she arrived she was shocked at how different the shop looked. The heavy commercial sewing machines used to sew parachutes and trousers were replaced by newer, sleeker models. The front window read Connie's Dress Shop.

"Constance?" Kay called from the doorway.

"Back here, Kay."

Kay made her way to the back room. She congratulated Harry. He accepted and quickly retreated into the front.

"I want to apologise for last night." Kay spoke to her turned back.

While Constance hadn't mentioned as much, Kay knew she was referring to herself when she'd talked about trading places. She'd been in love with Dick- truly in love with him. She knew Constance loved Harry and they'd be happy together, but her love affair with Dick would always leave a scar. A deep sadness over the baby and family which could've been- should've been.

"Thank you." Constance came over to embrace her. "We've been friends too long to let anything- even distance- come between us." Kay stepped back, blinking back tears and turned to glance at the front room.

"The shop looks great!"

"You think so? There's still so much to do. The machines will be back here. There will be fitting rooms just on the other side of this wall. Dresses on racks- and mannequins in the storefront."

"This is all so very exciting. When do I start?"

"Today if you'd like to."

So it was settled. Kay went to work every day for Constance and Harry. They were a happy pair. They worked together with hardly a squabble ever breaking out between them. Kay was surprised to see the babying which began during her previous pregnancy continued. He waited on her, fixing her tea and snacks. A new gold necklace and matching bracelet didn't go unnoticed either. He suited Constance and she suited him.

Days came and went. In early February, Ray came to visit with several G.I.'s scheduled for demobilisation. Piggy played the piano while everyone else sang along. They all stayed the night at Kay's and at dawn they left. Ray lagged behind wanting to say a personal goodbye away from the other men. Kay knew it may be the last she saw of Ray until her arrival in the States. He reassured her the arrangements for her travel were made and her movement details would arrive shortly by mail. While Kay accepted this fact, she was still in no hurry to leave England and her brothers behind. Tears ran down her face. Ray wiped them away.

"You'll be happy there. You'll see. You're gaining a mother and a father- a family."

"I know." She nodded her head. "I'll be there."

"Me, too. Waiting on the dock. I'll be counting the days between now and then."

He kissed Kay goodbye and held her tightly to him. He whispered into her ear.

"Be safe. God bless. I love you."

The following week Jonathan returned to Scotland to rejoin his wife and her family. Kay and the others stood on the station platform waving. It was the first of many goodbyes Kay knew must come. As the cold of February and March were replaced by the warmer temperatures of April, preparations for Constance's wedding were well underway.

Her dress was spectacular. The white overlaid silk was generously dotted with tiny seed pearls. The sleeves were short and puffy- in honour of spring. The bodice was fitted to the hips where it met a full skirt. There was an ornately decorated train at the back where it flowed as she walked down the aisle. Her father, now eighty, gingerly continued the short distance until arriving at the altar. His face conveyed the pride and happiness he felt on this day. Her mother was there as well, wearing a pale blue dress and matching jacket. On her head she wore a veiled hat. The only sadness for them all was the ongoing absence of her only brother Richard. They'd never heard from him in the months following the war and assumed him dead. Only Constance held out hope of someday hearing from him again.

Harry's love filled stare promised many things. She would be happy. She would be treasured. Most importantly she would be loved. Seeing them now made Kay recall her own wedding day to Ray. She'd felt all the same emotions. She'd felt loved. He would be a good husband and an even better father. This day marked a turning point for her as the last of her reluctance vanished.

She no longer feared her trip to the States- she embraced it! That night even though the reception lasted well into the early morning, she came home and began packing. The following morning a post arrived from the Embassy confirming her movement date of June 1st. The letter detailed many things. Among them were instructions for her suitcases. She would be permitted to have no more than two hundred pounds in luggage. She opted to pack a large trunk with her quilts, photographs and other non-personal items. It would be stored below deck due to limited space on board the ship. She would be permitted to keep two smaller sized suitcases in her possession which could be inspected if needed. On her person she should carry her Baptismal Record, as well as Marriage and Birth Certificates. Kay read through the letter carefully and scribbled notes about the various items required. She would have a few precious weeks to get all of them in order prior to her departure.

Train transportation was provided as was a warrant which would serve as a ticket for the entire trip. It was to be collected upon arrival at the final destination. All luggage and items needed to be tagged and marked. The list of instructions seemed endless. Kay worked with determination to set things in order. The suitcases would be easy to fill with room for only her nicest dresses, shoes, and a coat to wear onboard the ship, as well as various toiletries. The trunk, however, posed more of a challenge.

Her first attempt at filling the trunk resulted with it filled to overflowing, with an additional thirty or so other items remaining stacked on her bed. The task was a daunting one. There was no way she could bring everything. She laid across her bed surrounded by the clutter and closed her eyes.

"Need some help?"

The sight of Edith standing in the open door to her bedroom was a relief.

"I'm so glad you've come."

"Anthony thought you might need some help."

"He is correct in his thinking. I'm limited by weight. This

trunk should be sufficient but it isn't large enough for the number of items I have."

"But it will have to be or you risk coming in overweight?"

"Exactly."

"Well let's have a look here."

Edith walked over and gently started pulling the items out one at a time. She stopped short when she arrived at a stack of tablecloths large enough to cover an entire table ten times over.

"Must you really carry all of these?"

"I guess not- but there is one that is especially important to me."

"Then, we'll start there."

Kay selected the large, white antique tablecloth which had been her mum's. She folded it neatly and set it aside.

"I'll return the others to the cupboard."

"Perfect."

Edith disappeared from the room and returned empty handed.

"What next?"

"The large leather family Bible was my grandmum's and I'd like to fit it in."

"We'll need more room."

Edith approached the trunk and removed from it a few heavy jackets.

"These are certainly nice, but if you'll be carrying the other one onboard with you- you won't need these. Besides, they take up an enormous amount of space."

"I can part with the red one, but my mum sewed the other."

"That's a good compromise."

Edith looked at the red coat, longingly running her hand over it.

"Take it. I'd like you to have it."

"Really?"

"Certainly. Try it on."

Edith tried it on and it fit very nicely.

Kay walked over to the trunk and was now easily able to fit the family Bible into it. Enough space existed now to fit a few more of her things from the bed. The question would be what? A glance at the bed and there were still too many things to fit them all. Among them were three picture albums of family photos. The other items on the bed included her favourite quilt, more shoes, fabric, some jumpers, a mirror and comb set- as well as a surplus of clothing items.

"What else must go?"

"Everything already in the trunk I need. My wedding gown is in there- in pieces as it may be- but it's in there."

Kay walked around the bed. She'd already wrapped her father's pocketwatch in several handkerchiefs and hidden it away inside a shoe in one suitcase. Her mother's wedding band was secure on her right hand. Out of the remaining items the decision on what to carry with her was a simple one. She looked sadly at the comb and mirror set. They'd been a Christmas gift from her parents in happier times, but she knew they were not the sensible things to bring. Family photos were memories captured forever. She had no idea how long it'd be before she would be able to come home.

"The quilt and the picture albums must come with me."

"Let's do it then."

Edith took everything out of the trunk and neatly rearranged all of its contents. With some work, after thirty minutes she fit everything back inside plus the albums and quilt.

"If you'd like I think I can fit the comb and mirror in

between the folds of the quilt. It will protect the mirror some during travel."

"Splendid!"

Next Edith and Kay worked to close the trunk and return the other items to their proper places.

"You can have anything you would like Edith. The jumpers, the skirts- anything at all. Please come and take them all away after I leave."

"I will." Edith procured a tissue from her pocket and dabbed at her eyes. "You've been the only sister I've ever known. Having many brothers is not the same. Not the same at all."

Kay put her arm around Edith and gave her a squeeze.

"We're getting married." Edith announced between sniffles.

"I heard. Congratulations."

"I'm only sad you won't be here to witness it."

"I'll always be with you. Always."

Chapter Fourteen

It was nearing the end of the first week of their holiday and Christine, Kay, and Connie found themselves on yet another train- this time heading to Scotland. Her grandmother's brother, Jonathan, married a girl from Scotland after the war. They'd moved to a rural area outside Stirling where they'd lived happily and brought up three children. Jonathan had died many years ago, but Connie and Kay thought the holiday wouldn't be complete without visiting his family while they were here. His now grown children had young adult children of their own.

The first leg of the journey carried them into Edinburgh. The railway station was quite large and very busy. It was your typical large city. They didn't stay long and found themselves rushing to make their connection. Once onboard the smaller train bound for Stirling, Christine struck up a conversation with some local businessmen returning from a trip. It seemed the employment rate in Scotland was high and had been for quite some time. There was a time in the late nineties when many of the manufacturing plants once located there closed. Most of the unemployed at that time were young adults- some trade or even college educated. Since then things had changed, for the better, and Scotland was continuing to see job growth.

Christine thought of her own job and the workforce in the United States. She knew her own country had seen its share of ups and downs where the job market was concerned, but all in all she'd had a wonderful life. The American dream of owning your own business, building a home, and even overcoming seemingly insurmountable odds was still a possibility. She knew she was lucky to be living in her great country and that she had her grandmother to thank for it. After the conversation waned she studied the Scottish countryside. The landscape was a vivid green of rolling hills and far off mountains. Christine decided it was possibly the most beautiful land she'd ever seen in person. Her grandmother's soft voice beside her caught her attention.

"I came to visit my brother's family on my last visit. It was lovely- but this time we only have three days here. His daughters and son will be working during the day, but one of his son-in-laws has offered to drive us to visit the Queen Mother's childhood castle."

"I'd love that!"

"It isn't far from their house where we'll be staying. A little over an hours drive. It's in the highlands and I think you'll enjoy it."

"I know I will. We wanted to see it last time, but we ran out of time." Connie explained.

"Then, it's settled. We'll go tomorrow."

A short while later, they arrived at the station which was little more than a platform with a small building. A gentleman in his mid-forties named Neil greeted them. He was Kerry's husband, one of Jonathan's daughters. He loaded them quickly and helped them into the car. He set off at a fast clip and a short while later they were pulling into an amazing golf course. He explained his role in managing the golf course and how they lived in a farmhouse at the back of the property. The farmhouse dated back to the seventeen hundreds. This was fascinating to Connie and Christine.

The farmhouse was a simple wood frame building. Ivy grew up the walls obscuring them from view. It was large and had three full bedrooms on the second floor. The wood floors downstairs had been covered at some point with carpet. Christine would love to see what was underneath. The kitchen was large with a big iron stove still in the corner. More modern appliances and cabinetry were installed at some point but the original stove with its pipe venting to the outside added a rustic touch.

Neil advised Christine and his other guests not to drink the tap water as the pipes were made of lead. He said they used the water for cooking and showering- but to let it run a bit first. This would flush out the water sitting in the pipes which could possibly contain the highest concentration of lead. Christine wondered at the difficulty of repiping a farmhouse of this size, but decided it would be discourteous to ask. They'd obviously survived the lead pipes for years, but nonetheless she decided to limit the length of her showers.

The first evening they spent relaxing with Kerry and her sister. All of their adult children stopped by to say hello and meet them, but there were so many it was all a blur to Christine. There was a bar located in the club house where they all went to perform karaoke after dinner. Karaoke wasn't something she typically did. Before this trip, she'd sung karaoke perhaps twice in her entire lifetime. Now she found herself doing it twice in a week's time.

After the karaoke there was dancing. A small band made up of three older gentlemen played happy tunes. Christine found herself up and whirling around the small dance floor. Even her mother, who wasn't fond of dancing, rose to the occasion. Grandma- who required little convincing- led a line dance. The hours quickly passed and around three o'clock in the morning Christine slipped upstairs and pulled a piece of paper from her handbag. On it she wrote as many of the names as she could recall, as well as how each person was related to her. She slept soundly and awoke early the next morning when her mother's alarm clock sounded around seven o'clock.

"We need to get moving. This is our only full day here."
"I'm up."

Christine crawled from bed. Downstairs the kitchen was full of her Scottish cousins and laughter. Neil prepared an enormous breakfast and everyone was in great spirits- which was amazing considering the large quantity of spirits they'd all consumed only hours before. Grandma was there, sitting among them sipping her tea. Her bright eyes smiling and her cheery voice telling a story from long ago.

"Come join us, Christine. Your grandmum is just getting ready to tell the story about her and Dad- and the slasher during World War II."

"And this is funny?"

"You'll see- it is rather funny." Her grandmother patted the chair next to her in the crowded kitchen.

Christine came over and took a seat. Kerry set a steaming cup of black coffee down in front of her, a bowl of sugar, and some fresh cream.

"So, there we were in Manchester- Anthony and me. We were so used to being on our own by this time. All of my other brothers were off at war. Anthony and I worked two jobs- one sewing parachutes and another in a military factory. One evening, while we both happened to be off work- which was rare- Anthony went out with some mates. I, on the other hand, was still refusing to be social and attend parties or anything of the like with friends. I'd become quite the hermit- I think Christine would've called me a loner.

Well, this one evening I wanted candy. We'd gotten paid- hence the reason he was out with his mates. I tended to hoard my earnings unless of course it was something I wanted badly. Well, I wanted sweets. Candies were especially hard to come by since the Americans hadn't entered into the war yet- that came later. "

"What does Americans entering into the war have to do with candies?" One young cousin asked from near the kitchen counter.

"When the G.I.'s came they brought with them chocolate, candy, cigarettes- even coffee. It was like Christmas, but better. So anyhow- my brothers warned me against going out after dark. A young woman alone in wartime England- it was dangerous. Of course, there were bombings, but it was a desperate time. Many people lost everything they had- their homes- their belongings. The streets were unsafe at night for a multitude of reasons. So there I was- craving sweets. The only shop I knew still open which sold them was down near the warf- which for me was a bit of a walk. Against my own better judgement I decided to walk there anyhow- alone- to buy some.

On the way there, I passed this man leaning against a light pole. He didn't lift his head in acknowledgment and was wearing a trench coat. I heard him begin to follow me so I began to walk quite quickly to the store. The only problem was once there I would have to walk back. Now, you have to remember, this is before cell phones and we didn't even have a home phone. So, I bought the candy and stayed inside the shop until it closed. When I came outside, he was no where in sight. I thought the coast was clear.

I started back down the street- now it was very dark outside. There were streetlights but the bulbs were all hooded so the light shined straight down- this way there was little visible light from overhead for bombers to target. While this spared us from being bombed some of the time, it served as camouflage for pick pockets and such. So, there I am, speed walking my way home. I heard footsteps behind me and turned to see who it was. A man- the same one from before- darted out from behind a corner. I started walking faster. So did he. I started running. So did he.

At last, I made it to my door. I unlocked it and ran inside- latching it behind me. My windows were all blacked out. I heard someone outside the front door- trying the latch. I ran and hid myself inside a cupboard downstairs. Suddenly, I thought to the back door. I hadn't taken time to check the lock. I couldn't be sure it was secure. I heard the footsteps on my front porch and then he walked around the side of my house. My neighbour's dog was barking incessantly. He knew all of our friends and my brothers. He never barked. I knew then it was the man in the trench coat who'd followed me home.

He tried the back door. I heard the handle going up and down- I wasn't sure if he'd gotten in. There was a slasher who all the towns people were calling a Jack the Ripper copycat. He'd been grabbing girls walking home alone, at night. It was in all the papers and we were all terrified- making sure to never walk home from the factories alone. Suddenly, I heard the front door open and close. The footsteps crossed the house and stopped in front of the cupboard. The lights were out and the house was still black. I armed myself with the broom handle and swung the door open hitting the intruder with the force of it. I swung in the darkness, whacking him on the back and the neck with the broom handle- sending him to the floor. I didn't stop until he lay unconscious on the floor in the dark. It turns out it was my brother Jonathan home on furlow!"

The room erupted with laughter.

"That's one heck of a greeting, Auntie Kay !" Kerry laughed.

"I guess so. I felt quite badly about it, but he should've announced it was him."

"He loved you so. He said he'd always remember you that way. The little sister who was as tough as any mate and could hold her own."

"What about the slasher?" Christine slid forward to the edge of her seat.

"He killed another girl that very night. The description matched the man who had followed me. Jonathan verified seeing him walking out of our back ally when he approached our house. He'd gotten a bad feeling off him. Suffice to say- I never went out unattended after dark again."

"After Grandma's harrowing tale about the slasher I don't think I will either!" Christine admitted.

Everyone finished breakfast and walked them out. The car only sat four and with Neil driving there wasn't room for anyone else. The trip to Glamis Castle was longer than she'd thought it would be but was well worth the trip over. The sprawling expanse of green pasture and grazing Highland Hereford cattle greeted them as they passed through the gates. The castle itself was breathtaking and while only two wings were open for visitation, they were spectacular. The other areas were reserved for use by the Royal family and Christine found herself wanting to sneak over to tour those as well.

The tour guide shared stories about the castle, its history and its ghosts. In one story she told of a vampire child who was born to the family every few generations or so. In another she told about an entire family who walled themselves up in the castle in an attempt to escape their enemies. As a result the thick wall was still in place and the family starved to death behind it. She referred to it as *The Room of Skulls*. Christine glanced to her grandmother who whispered

"The wall story is true indeed and quite sad. As for the vampire story- I think that's absolute rubbish. There couldn't be any truth in it."

After the tour ended they decided a light lunch in the eatery downstairs would be nice. Christine, Connie, and her grandmother selected bottled waters, a cheese wedge, and egg salad sandwiches for their meal.

"I'd like to see the gardens. I received a post card from

Jonathan's wife years ago and was astounded by their beauty."

"I'd like to see them too." Connie attested.

So it was settled. The ladies finished their lunch and threw the rubbish away. Out in the main section of the castle they stopped off at the visitor's desk for a map of the property. The weather was quite damp outside and the attendant informed them there wouldn't be many visitors to the gardens today due to the cancellation of the tour. This made no difference to Christine or the others, so they set off- map in hand- in search of the garden.

Once outside, they proceeded along the side of the castle towards the general direction where the gardens were located. The path was not paved and the grass was quite deep- and wet. As their quest to find the gardens continued Christine became sure they'd taken a wrong turn. They were now several yards from the castle and no where near a garden of any sort, unless you considered open pasture a garden of sorts. Just then Christine became aware of movement to her right. She glanced over her shoulder and saw the entire herd of Highland Herefords heading straight for them. They were running full out and in the back of her mind all Christine could think of was the stampedes of the old Westerns.

They were still walking and in the distance Christine could see a tall fence overgrown with green foliage. It was a mere fifty yards away. In that moment she was thankful for her grandmother's youthful continence.

"Cows!" Christine screamed.

She and her mother exchanged a panicked look. Her mother grabbed grandma's arm on one side and Christine did the same on the other side.

Was it just her imagination or were these the largest cattle she'd ever seen? They were taller than their American counterparts and their fur was extremely long and shaggy. It hung in clumps all over their bodies. The thundering of their hooves could now be felt on the ground and they were almost upon them.

Christine ran to the garden gate and swung it open for her grandmother and mom. Both sprinted in, followed by Christine who swung it closed behind her. A dozen large cows ran right up to the gate and screeched to a halt. They looked disappointed.

"I think they thought we came to feed them." Her grandmother admitted. "I don't think they meant us any harm."

"Or they were hungry and they thought we were food."

Christine teased. "Regardless- my holiday plans never included getting trampled by a herd of stampeding cattle."

"Well, now we're in here- we better stay put for a while. They don't look like they're going anywhere."

"I'd wanted to hike in the surrounding woods. Maybe if we hide out in here they'll forget about us and go away."

They turned and began their exploration of the garden. The Italian style garden was full of rhododendrons and azaleas still in bloom. The other more sensitive flowers such as daffodils, primroses, and violets wouldn't bloom again until spring. There were native plants of the hearty variety which appeared unaffected by the recent changes in temperature. The foxglove, thistle, and teasel were vibrant and full of life.

Christine longed to pick an azalea to take home and press between the pages of a well-loved book, but she suppressed the desire. She and her grandmother walked along the neatly trimmed yew hedges following walkways towards a pristinely manicured lawn. There they took a seat on a wrought iron bench and enjoyed the view of the fountain.

"We return to Wigan tomorrow." Christine announced.

"Yes, then we'll visit Manchester the following day. After that we return home in two days time."

"It must be hard saying goodbye, Grandma- I can't even imagine it."

"That's the reason we do those things when we're young. If asked to do it at an old age we'd be far too cautious and wise to even consider it- though Abraham didn't seem to have that problem."

"You wouldn't do it all over again if you had the chance?"

"Oh- I would. It's just age makes us more hesitant and fearful. I'm glad I didn't know fear then- I was fearless. Sure I had moments of doubt- reluctance even. It took courage to leave my family and country behind, but I did it and I'm glad I did. I tried to turn back at the station but in the end my brothers' support and common sense won out. I knew your grandfather awaited me. And with him a new life- a better life than I could have without him. I remember trying to imagine a life without him- falling in love with someone else for me would have proven impossible. He was the love of my life and in many ways he still is. He's waiting for me you know. Just like he waited for me then, he waits for me now. This time his wait has been much longer, but he knows I'm coming. "

"I think your brothers and parents are waiting for you, too."

"I know they are. I'm not in any hurry to go mind you- but when it's my time I'm ready. I've lived a long, wonderful life."

Chapter Fifteen

May 16, 1946

Kay boarded the train among tear filled goodbyes and riotous cheers from her brothers. She was shaking from a mixture of nerves and fright. At the last moment she tried to turn back but George stopped her, a gentle hand on her shoulder.

"We love you, but you must go. Ray needs you and you need him. Be happy, Katie ."

She willed her feet to climb the steps and walked down the centre aisle to her seat. She removed her jacket and folded it across her arm. She slid across to her seat and placed her pocketbook next to her. The train was nearly full and she could feel it beginning to move. From her window seat, Kay waved until Anthony, George, and Billy faded from sight. Even Theresa and Edith came to bid her farewell. While both girls tried to hide the tears, she saw them running down their cheeks. She looked away trying to hold on to the inner control she'd found this morning.

She was on her way to the army barracks where she'd spend the next five days until her voyage departed for the States. She didn't know what to expect. Her brothers each gave her pocket money for any incidentals she might need. Some time into the trip she fell asleep. When the train stopped, she'd arrived at the station where a bus would carry her the remaining distance to the camp.

The barracks were abuzz with activity. There must have been over four hundred war brides similar to her. She was guided to an office where she stood in line to show her letter and the required paperwork. After more than two hours in line, it was her turn. Everything went well and she was assigned to a bunkhouse shared with fifteen other women. She was excited to meet a young woman named Bernice who was from Wigan. After a few minutes of conversation, they learned they knew some of the same people.

Bernice's husband was an army soldier from South Carolina. Some of the other women were married to men who were from western states such as Wyoming and even California. They provided Kay with the details of their trips and final destinations. It turns out the boat would be only the first leg of the journey for many of them, but not for Kay . The USS Saturnia would carry her to Ellis Island, where Ray would be picking her up and driving her the remaining distance to North Brookfield, Massachusetts.

Over the course of the next week, Kay and the other women underwent multiple physical examinations checking for everything from lice to venereal disease. Shot records were verified and fingerprints taken. Their luggage was searched and while all of these things were tiring, most of the girls didn't seem to mind. An overall feeling of excitement and joy in the prospect of seeing their husbands in the near future propelled them forward.

Finally, the day for departure arrived. Kay and Bernice caught the train with all of the other war brides to Southampton. From there they were taken to the dock where the USS Saturnia awaited them. She'd never seen a ship this large before. To Kay it was downright enormous. Boarding the women, their suitcases and other luggage took quite a long time. After several hours, Kay busied herself in her cabin with eleven other women. She slid her suitcases under the bunk, as there was no room for them in the small cupboard already filled to overflowing with her cabinmates' cases. The other women seemed exceptionally warm and hospitable, travelling from all over Europe to make the trip.

Bernice's room was just down the hall. When Kay finished stowing her luggage she went in search of her. Bernice looked to be finishing up when Kay entered her cabin. They could feel the giant engines of the ship come on and Kay knew there was no turning back now. She and Bernice shared a knowing look for a moment which was quickly replaced by smiles. Kay took Bernice by the arm and escorted her out of their room and to the Mess Hall.

Life onboard the ship was routine. Breakfast first thing in the morning, followed by a grand lunch, and dinner at six o'clock in the evening. The food was rich indeed. The first night Kay feasted on sirloin steak, pole beans, bread and butter, tomato bisque soup, fresh salad, and apple pie for dessert. The other meals were just as delectable. While Kay stomached the sea well, others were not as fortunate. The savoury meals filled with cream and buttery sauces were too heavy for many of their stomachs and they found themselves quite sick.

Most evenings Kay spent caring for an ill Bernice. She suffered greatly with sea sickness. Kay felt for her and did her best to ease her queasiness by placing cold compresses on the nape of her neck and forehead. After a few days Bernice seemed to be settling in better and wasn't as sick. The only lingering effects from the illness seemed to come right after breakfast. Kay wondered if Bernice might be expecting a child, but didn't ask. Bernice made no mention of it and she must have her reasons for not sharing if she were indeed pregnant.

The canteen, located on the second floor of the ship, proved to be a tremendous amount of fun. There Kay purchased a silver lighter to give to Ray upon her arrival. There were sweets and make-up. She decided to buy a small gift for her mother-in-law as well. Ma had been so kind in sending the lace and silk stockings. As a result, Kay didn't want to arrive empty handed. She sampled several of the perfumes and after a short time selected a sweet smelling one. She dabbed a bit from the tester onto her wrists and the nape of her neck. It smelled of jasmine and citrus. It was a refreshingly sweet combination. She'd love to receive this as a gift herself and knew therefore it would be perfect for Ma. Bernice bought herself some make-up including a new eyebrow pencil and lipstick.

Each evening the girls would watch a movie. The ship seemed to offer all the amenities they'd been without these past years. The voyage was quickly becoming more of a holiday cruise rather than the mere transport it served as. That night after they'd gone to sleep, Kay awoke when the violent rocking of the ship tossed her nearly out of bed. Several others sat up in the darkness discussing the gale.

"It seems we're in a bad storm." Brenda voiced her complaint from overhead.

"I felt it. The waves must be tremendous."

"I don't want to see it."

"Me neither. I'm glad we've no windows."

Kay staggered out of her bunk and grabbed the rubbish bin from the corner of the room near the cupboard. She set it in front of Agatha who looked as if she might need it any moment. She nodded her head in thanks, but was too ill to speak. The seas rolled until midmorning at which point everyone staggered to the deck to take in some fresh air. Kay located Bernice. She didn't look well either.

"Are you all right?"

"I think I will be. We've only three days left on this wretched ship."

"Why don't you go lie down for a bit. I'll bring your lunch to you."

"Thank you."

Bernice clutched her abdomen and walked holding onto the guardrail for dear life. A few hours later Kay went to her cabin carrying a tray. She'd selected the vegetable soup, bread, cheese, and apple wedges. She knew from experience they would be the easiest to hold down and work to quell Bernice's upset stomach.

When Kay entered, Bernice was fast asleep. The light from the hallway shined in on her causing her to stir. She rolled over and opened her eyes a little at Kay's approach.

"Thank you, Kay. You're a Dear." She glanced around the room and saw no one was present. She began to speak freely. "I'm pregnant you know. Just under four months. They didn't detect it during the exams and I lied."

"Why would you do that?"

"I wouldn't have been able to travel until after the baby came. And as far as ships go this one is top-notch...not at all like the disease filled nightmares I've heard reports of."

"Disease filled?"

"Yes, Kay. Some of the early reports were downright disturbing. Horrid conditions. Missing railing on the decks, confiscated baby food and formula. I've heard of cases where infants have even died. I figured I'd rather take my chances travelling pregnant on a fantastic ship than on a bad one with a small infant or toddler."

Kay's thoughts immediately went to Mary and young Molly. They'd travelled a few months before her. She'd heard nothing of them since. She feared for their well being but thought it best not to borrow trouble. She silently prayed for them both, especially Molly, making the sign of the cross.

"You've known someone travelling with a child?" When Kay merely blinked at her, not giving an answer Bernice apologised. "I shan't have said as much as I have."

"No- I'm glad you did. I will look them up as soon as I arrive. As for you- no more out and about. Some bed rest and lots of fluids. You've only three days to go. We're going to get you there in top shape. You'll see."

That night Kay prayed for smoother seas and a calm, uneventful trip. She and Bernice did very little other than lounge around in her bunk. Each evening they ventured as far as dinner and the evening movie. On the eve of their arrival Kay wouldn't allow Bernice to lift even a finger. She packed her suitcases for her and set out her change of clothing for the morning's arrival. The girls exchanged addresses knowing in the morning they may not see each other and if they did they might not have time for proper goodbyes. One last hug and a quick goodbye was all there was time for before lights out. Kay wished Bernice well and God speed on the rest of her journey.

She made her way to her own cabin and packed her items away. She'd done most of the packing earlier and was thankful she'd taken the time. She set out her favourite royal blue skirt with a silk blouse with white delicate beading. She'd saved her silk stockings and heels for this occasion. She pin curled her hair in the dark-something she'd gotten good at during the war. She decided to be as well turned out for this reunion with Ray as she could possibly be.

It'd been months since they parted and she was far more excited to see him than she'd imagined possible. That night she fell fast asleep, a smile gracing her lips. At dawn she'd be reunited with her one true love and the thought put both her mind and soul at ease.

All of the other women were fussing about well before dawn. Their movements, along with the flickering light, alerted Kay to the time. She took care removing her pins and fluffing her hair. She applied some of her new make-up and dressed. All of the women came on deck to watch the USS Saturnia pull into New York Harbour and make its approach to Ellis Island. The Statue of Liberty was clearly visible. Her arm raised, torch extending into the sky. The women had heard of the splendor and greatness of her majesty but until this moment none had experienced it. The beauty of her flowing robes and wreathed head brought tears slipping down their faces.

The great ship docked and every woman worked to haul her luggage off. Soldiers were there assisting them. Kay made no rush to get caught up in the commotion. Rather she stood motionless staring at the New York City skyline rising in the distance and the harbour stretching out before her. She knew this land to be a vast one, filled with large cities, small towns, rolling hillsides, and great mountains. This country was hers and she'd make it her own. When the crowd tapered down to less than a hundred or so remaining passengers, a soldier approached her asking if she needed assistance. She gladly accepted.

She walked down the plank and saw Ray standing on the dock, his hat held in his hands. Over his arm he carried a mink fur coat and a small gift box tied with a bow. She ran to meet him and was lost in his embrace. They kissed and then they cried, holding each other. The years of war, time, distance, and separation all just came to an end. Beside them the soldier set her cases down and disappeared back to the ship. Ray and Kay, oblivious to the world around them, kissed the time away so glad to be back in each others arms.

When Kay lifted her head she saw they weren't alone. Embarrassed, she blushed a bright crimson.

"Kay, this is Francis, my cousin."

Kay shook the young man's extended hand and smiled sweetly at him.

"You'll have to excuse us. It's been a while since we've seen each other."

"Don't apologise, Miss. Let me grab your bags. I'll meet you two at the ferry. Don't lag behind too long- you'll miss the ferry altogether."

Francis disappeared down the docks towards the ferry. When he was out of sight Ray handed Kay the fur coat.

"I figured your other coats may have been too heavy to pack."

"They were. You're so thoughtful."

Ray assisted her in slipping it on and she delighted in the fact it fit perfectly. Next Ray handed her the small gift box. She removed the bow and ribbon. Inside it held a small, gold scarf pin. The pin was delicate and had a small basket attached to it. The basket had a hinged door which opened and closed. Kay opened it. Inside it concealed a gold pair of diamond stud earrings. Upon closer inspection she discovered the diamonds were set in gold stars.

Kay put the earrings on and neatly pinned the pin to her blouse. Francis waved and called wildly from the end of the dock. They held hands and sprinted to catch the ferry. They arrived just in time and slowly made their way across to the mainland with the many others.

At Ray's parents' home, a small welcome party awaited them. Kay met his brother and a few cousins, as well as his sister Patricia. Ma was there as well and wanted to hear all about Kay's voyage over. She inquired about the half finished dress and within moments convinced Kay they'd be able to finish it in time for the summer wedding she'd originally envisioned. The dogwoods would be in bloom and the air would be warm and sweet.

The following day they opened her trunk and brought out the bridal gown, which was carefully stowed inside. Its bodice, skirt, sleeves, and veil all lay in pieces. She'd removed the straight pins for the trip not sure whether or not they'd be permitted on the boat. Ma began the task of laying the pieces out on the dining table. Kay pinned each piece in place. After half an hour, they'd pieced together what was beginning to resemble a dress. Kay hand stitched the skirt and the train onto the back, while Ma fashioned the lace eyelets for the bustle and sewed them in place. Next, Kay switched her focus to the bodice where she attached the sleeves.

Ma began work on the long, lace veil Kay described. It must flow to nearly the middle of her back. Around the face she wanted scalloped lace. On the veil itself she requested tatted lace flowers with seed pearl accents. Hours turned to days, and days into weeks, and all the while the two women sewed. One morning it finally came time to fit the dress. When they did it was exquisite. Kay knew her summer ceremony would be just as special as the one she'd originally wanted back in England. As the day drew closer Betsy, Robert's wife and her new sister-in-law, visited her more frequently. With her she brought the photo album of her own wedding ceremony. The decorations and wedding reception were of an elegant fashion. The brunch was held outdoors at an apple orchard. The bridesmaids carried roses and wore pale pink dresses. Even in Kay's dreams she'd never envisioned such splendor. Her anticipation of her own day and all it could be grew. Her life was a dream- a fantastic dream- and she was living it.

Chapter Sixteen

The train lurched to a halt. Christine and her grandmother unloaded at Manchester Station. Connie opted to remain behind in Wigan spending one last day with her cousins there. Christine and Kay grabbed their small overnight bags, stepped off the train, and walked towards the exit leading out onto the street.

"Shall we get a cab?"

"No. It's not far and I'd like to walk. There's something I'd like to show you along the way."

Christine slung her small tote over her shoulder and took her grandmother's as well. Knowing how fond her grandmother was of walking, she'd donned her comfortable trainers- a few moments later she was thankful she had. They made their way through the area of town near the docks where her grandmother once worked in the factories. The area was freshly redone and most of it didn't resemble what it looked like before. Still her grandmother was able to point out exactly where things once stood. They continued through town and towards the old shopping district.

The building which once had been Harry's still stood but the shop had long since been replaced by a barrister's office. Manchester was quite large, especially if a person intended on covering it on foot. Christine realised how spoiled she was with her American dependence on cars. She was panting like a puppy while Grandma seemed to be taking everything in stride, outpacing her every step of the way.

Halfway up another street they passed the building where the dances were housed- it was still standing and other than a fresh coat of paint looked virtually the same. Next they turned and crossed several city blocks until they arrived at Oxford Road and the original location of the Church of the Holy Name where she and Ray were first married. The church was closed and they were not able to go inside. Just the same they shared a silent prayer, then Grandma described in detail her daily mass attendance there with her mother before she died. She was proud to still attend mass everyday, something her mother had instilled in her at an early age. Some things can't be taken away- not by time, war, or the closing of a building. Certain traditions remain and continue.

Next they turned and walked the short distance to the location where her home stood on Plymouth Street. Their eyes were met by new homes. Christine reached over and held her grandmother's hand.

"When your mother and I visited several years ago we arrived to find my old home was gone. It'd survived war only to be torn down over twenty years later for new construction. Life goes on. Out with the old and in with the new- but I still have my memories."

"And what amazing memories they are."

"Let's stop in at the Plymouth Grove Hotel for old time's sake and have a beer."

Christine followed as Kay led the way to the Plymouth Grove Hotel. Inside they took a seat at the bar. Christine got the definite feeling they were stalling for some reason but didn't dare ask the reason. She drank her pint and afterwards they continued their journey to Anthony's home. He was the last living brother to her grandmother and she knew this may be the last time she saw him alive.

At his door she knocked loudly and he came within a few moments to answer it. He was still youthful and agile- Christine was relieved to see it ran in the family. He led them to the kitchen where he had tea waiting for them. Warm fish and chips with curry sauce sat in the middle of the small dining table.

"It's been a long time since I've had proper fish and chips." Kay announced.

She pulled out her chair and began fixing herself a plate. Christine glanced around Anthony's small, compact kitchen. It was crammed full of china, pots and pans. The tiny space was filled to overflowing but in spite of its size and the number of items occupying all available space, it was tidy. Anthony waited on them, fixing them each a soda and setting the table with additional napkins.

"Where's Edith?"

"She stepped out for a bit. She needed a few things at market but should be back shortly."

Christine quickly recalled her grandmother's stories and Edith. She'd been but a young woman when her grandmother left, vowing to forever be with her. They must have seen each other on the other two visits, but so far her grandmother made no mention of it. Christine wondered how she'd changed. Was she in good health? So many of her grandmother's friends had died and still she was upbeat. She didn't let the things of this world bother her. The front door chimed and Christine knew it must be Edith who entered the house.

Christine stood to move around to the chair at the back of the table against the wall but halted when a spritely woman of seventy or so practically skipped into the room. Christine stood in awe of her. Her salt and pepper hair pulled high into a chignon at the top of her head. Feathery wisps of hair fell around her face. Her cheeks were rosy and full of colour, as were her lips. On her face she wore not an ounce of make-up but she still looked youthful and exuberant. In her arms she easily carried three bags full of fresh bread, butter, and milk. She was wearing a pair of lightweight trainers and looked to have walked all the way to and from the market.

Everything about Edith conveyed happiness and joy. Christine felt it radiate off her and felt elated from the mere proximity, as if she were absorbing this woman's positive energy. Anthony was just as high energy. He gave his wife a kiss on the cheek and patted her backside lightly. He spoke about their grown children and grands. It seems they were all quite jovial and upbeat- inheriting from their parents the same love of life. Christine was surprised to hear them talk about their fast approaching holiday to Malta. It was something they worked to do every year. Usually all of their children and great-grandchildren went along as well.

The more Christine sat and listened to them, the more she wanted what they had. Her grandfather had died relatively young due to heart complications. Still her grandmother travelled and went dancing quite frequently. She was surrounded by loving family and loads of friends- but what Edith and Anthony had was something entirely different. They had each other- even in old age. She wondered if it bothered her grandmother to have lost her grandfather so young. Later that night, in the privacy of the bedroom they shared, she decided to ask her.

"Grandma, do you ever get sad with Papa being gone?"

"Oh- of course. I wish he'd lived longer but my mother used to say we live life as it is- not the way we wish it to be. That's why it's so important to live each day as if it were your last. It sounds cliched but it's true. Losing my parents and brother Jimmy the way I did taught me that."

"I need to work on that. I've just been sort of wandering through life. Not really appreciating everything I've been blessed with. My parents, my siblings- even you."

"It's never too late to begin anew. And let's not forget Jeff. You've been blessed with a man who loves you and wants to spend the rest of his life with you. That is truly a blessing indeed- one you should never take for granted."

"What happened after you arrived in the States?"

"We lived life. A wonderful, full life."

Christine lay in silence thinking about the simplicity of those words...*we lived life.* What did they mean exactly? Before she thought on it further her grandmother continued.

"We moved to the country, a quaint little country cottage. I got a pony, and was pregnant almost immediately. We had two of the four girls while we lived on the small farm. I remember getting chickens and collecting fresh eggs every morning- something I never got during the war. Fresh eggs! I still remember it. Your grandfather built me a chicken coop. The girls loved it as well. There wasn't anywhere to walk to- we truly lived in the country. Your grandfather's family still owned the airfield and sometimes I'd lead the girls down the dirt roads the three miles to it and back again. We were happy.

Occasionally our friends, Mary and Joe, would come to visit us. Their little girl Molly turned out to be a beautiful little girl- but was quite the brat- always taking your mother's toys and such." Her grandmother paused to laugh about that part of it now. "I always thought they got on spectacularly well- Mary and Joe- and was shocked when I learned they divorced twenty years later. I lost touch with them when they divorced- each going their separate ways.

I won't say my marriage was perfect- because marriage never is. There are lows and there are highs- but in the end it is a beautiful thing. It is the journey of marriage that makes it beautiful- whether it lasts only a few years or a lifetime. I wish I'd had him longer but I have always been thankful to have had him at all. Thirty-two years is a long time. We shared many a dance during that time. Boy, could your grandfather dance! He played the guitar as well.

His parents sold the airfield when I was pregnant with your Aunt Teri and we moved to south Florida. He took a job working for the airport and I took a job baking in the school cafeteria. While it wasn't my own pastry shop- I was the head cook and I ran the place in first-rate fashion. I never learned to drive although I have to credit you with trying to teach me when you were a teenager."

"I remember."

"How could you forget? I thought I really had the hang of it right up until the point where I put that golfcart through your mother's garage door."

"Yes- the telltale hole was evidence of our driving lesson for weeks until Daddy got it repaired. I figured teaching you to drive was the least I could do to repay all of those dance lessons. I was the only four year old who could waltz, jitterbug, and Charleston."

"When the girls were all little I used to do something I called the Silly Half Hour."

"The Silly Half Hour?"

"It's just what it sounds like. We'd dress in costumes, sometimes just wear aprons and hats. We'd march and sing, beat on pots and pans with spoons- it was fun. All in all I was thankful they'd never wake to air raid sirens or be afraid to go to sleep. They were happy and carefree- the way children should be. Don't begrudge the fact that your life has been an easy one- be grateful."

"I am. Thank you, Grandma, for teaching me the real meaning of marriage."

Her grandmother reached over and lightly held her hand.

"I'd been so caught up in the dress, the flowers, the cake, the rehearsal dinner. It was nearly robbing my enjoyment of the whole thing, but when it comes down to it this one day is merely a small part of it all. It is just one day. It is the actual day-in and day-out of marriage which makes it what it is. The children, the fights, the faith- the living. I've spent too much time not really living. My living begins right now. I want to dance in the kitchen with pots and pans- I want a Silly Half Hour! I think we all deserve that and no less. Jeff deserves a woman who is eager to marry him- a woman who is eager to make him happy and create happiness for herself too. I've been a bum- a real bum. Just sort of existing- well, no more. You can't be happy, truly happy with a mere existence."

"I think you're on to something. My aunt always told me

marriage is never fifty- fifty. Sometimes it's thirty-seventy. Sometimes it's forty-sixty. Sometimes you're the one doing more than your share- sometimes it's your spouse who's doing all the work. And I don't mean at the office. It's those times when you learn what defines you. In our family, it's perseverance and commitment. We don't give up easily. You're from a long line of women who are tough, strong and resilient. If you go into marriage expecting anything less than a battle at times- you're kidding yourself. There are good times of course, but there will be bad times too. Embrace the good times and work through the bad- that's marriage."

"What about Bernice?"

"Bernice and I have been pen pals our entire lives. She went on to have six children and was very happily married. She lives in San Fernando with her husband- I've even gone out to visit her through the years. She's ended up being a lifelong friend. Who would have thought it? We grew up less than thirty miles from one another and never met. Then we meet on a warship as war brides- we became pen pals and have been friends for forty plus years."

Her grandmother spoke with such deep sentiment and emotion it could be felt in every word she uttered.

Christine thought about her grandmother's other friends. Hilda, Veronica, Theresa, Susan, and the others who died through the years. She, Edith and Constance were all that were left of her group of childhood friends. Constance and Harry went on to have three boys and lived a very happy life together. He'd died a few years earlier due to cancer but was survived by their three children and several grandchildren, as well as twelve great-grandchildren. Constance never learned what happened to her brother in France. As it turns out, through the years she and Harry made several trips there in search of him, even hiring a private investigator. Later in life Constance became a woman of great faith, as a result she knew someday she would see Richard again.

That evening lying in bed, Christine discovered a new appreciation for her own friends- friends like Vanessa whom she'd known since high school. They graduated and opted to attend college where they'd chosen to room together even after graduation. They were now both engaged and getting married. She would be moving to upstate New York with her husband, who'd already relocated there with his job. While it never seemed to matter before- it suddenly became hugely important to keep in touch. Vanessa was always a part of her life. It was up to Christine to make sure it remained that way. Neither time nor distance separated her grandmother and Constance. With modern communications, it would be easy to do. Christine couldn't imagine having communicated all those years via snail mail. Not only with Constance but with her brothers, their wives, and now their children and great-grandchildren. Then there were the cousins, aunts, and even uncles to consider. Her grandmother managed to keep in touch with them all. She was truly an amazing woman.

Grandma yawned lightly and Christine decided it would be best to let her go to sleep for the night. Christine thought about how she could better live each day. How she could make a difference in her life and in others' lives as well.

The next morning they enjoyed a light breakfast and were on their way to the airport. Connie would be meeting them there. When they arrived at the airport Christine was surprised at how much of their family came to bid them farewell. Edith and Anthony brought them goodbye gifts of British teas not yet available in the States and matching teacups. Their goodbyes were tearful ones, but in her grandmother she sensed an excitement to be returning home. They wheeled their luggage into the check-in area. Grandma suggested a quick shopping spree in the duty free area to purchase small touristy gifts for all of their family back home.

"You all right?" Connie asked Grandma as they browsed the shop.

"I am. It was hard the first time I left them all behind, but when I went *home* to visit eighteen years later I realised the United States had become my home. England will always be the place of my childhood and so many fond memories- but I no longer consider it home. It's nice to visit, but it's nice to go *home*. I miss my bed."

Christine cracked up at her grandmother's unabashed honesty. Christine missed her bed too. She missed her bed and her cocker spaniel, Joy. She missed her small apartment and her garden tub- but most importantly she missed Jeff. Grandma was right. He was a great guy and he loved her. She perused the shop shelves and found a Manchester rugby hat she thought he'd like. She tried it on for size and decided matching hats might be even better. Next she located a small teapot for her sister. It was a one cup and contained a built-in tea strainer for loose leaf tea. Her sister loved tea and she knew it would be perfect for her. Finally she found a beer mug which she decided would fit nicely in her father's collection. Satisfied with her selections she made her way to the register.

Outside the three of them continued in silence towards their boarding gate. Christine's overall feeling was bittersweet. She knew on the one hand she'd shared something with her mother and grandmother most young people never get the opportunity to do and that made her happy. On the other hand she was sad. Her grandmother was getting older. They all acknowledged this may be her last trip. While she considered the United States her home she seemed to enjoy the visit while they were here. Christine only wished it weren't so far.

On the plane she found she slept with ease- most likely due to pure exhaustion. When she stirred at the announcement they'd soon be landing in Orlando she had to physically wake both her mother and grandmother. Their trip came to an end but in it she found a new connection with her grandmother which could never be severed. As the women left the aeroplane and walked down to baggage claim, Christine saw a long-legged frame standing next to the luggage carousel holding a sign among all of the other chauffeurs and transport groups. It read *Christine.*

Jeff was always good for a laugh. She ran over and threw her arms around him realizing just how much she'd missed him over the past two weeks and how much more she wanted to marry the man standing in front of her. She kissed him on the lips and clung tightly to him.

"I'm glad you're home, too."

He set her down and went over to help Connie and Kay with their luggage as well. Carol was there as well, hugging each of them, welcoming them home.

"How was it, ladies?"

"We had fun but we sure are glad to be home." Grandma groaned. "I wonder what they've been doing at the Legion while I was gone. That Phyllis wants my job as lead kitchen cook but she can't do the job the way I do. We've got a dance there tomorrow. I'm expecting nearly two hundred for dinner. Let's head home Jeff, where I can get some rest before I drive into work tomorrow."

"The Legion is supposed to be fun Mom- not work." Connie cut her eyes at Christine and Carol.

"Who are you kidding? It is fun. I cook for men who appreciate it and get to have someone else clean up the kitchen afterwards. Then comes the dancing- of course I'm not really interested in any of those old coots but it's still fun to get out there and cut a rug."

"Sounds fun, Grandma."

"You and your young man will have to come some time. You'll love it."

"I'm sure we would." Jeff grinned.

Jeff winked at Christine and Christine knew it meant he was more than serious about taking Grandma up on her offer of dancing at the Legion. He drove her mother home first. Then dropped her grandmother and sister off as well. By the time Christine got home she was ready to eat dinner and get showered. He helped her in with her luggage and kissed her goodbye. It was late Sunday evening and he needed to be at work first thing in the morning.

Inside, Christine found her wedding dress laid out neatly across her bed. She walked over and smoothed her hand softly down the front folds. She went into her cupboard and fetched the veil she'd purchased before her trip and was surprised to see how nicely they complimented each other. The sequins and pearls were an exact match. While the bodice of the gown was entirely covered in both, only the outside edges of the veil were adorned in the sequins and pearls. Both the dress and veil were off white. If she hadn't been so tired she would've tried them on together, but it would have to wait for another day. She went into her bathroom where she ran her bath full of hot water and lavender Epsom salts. An hour later she emerged relaxed and ready to sleep. She would need to be at work tomorrow bright and early where she was sure a pile of emails awaited her. You didn't get to be a theme park Customer Service Manager without working your tail off and she knew her absence wouldn't make a difference in the operation. It ran three hundred sixty-five days a year, whether she was on holiday or not. She climbed into bed and pulled her quilt up to her nose.

Chapter Seventeen

Over the next several months, Christine set to work finalising her wedding plans. It became quite simple after her conversations with Grandma. The focus changed from the event to the ceremony, the vows and the family and friends who would be travelling from all over to share their special day. For flowers she decided to combine her favourite off white roses and Baby's Breath alongside strands of ivy cascading down from the arrangement. For her bridesmaids, she opted to simplify things and have only her sister on the altar with her. For ushers, Jeff called in a bunch of his fraternity brothers, making sure the most handsome would escort her grandmother down the aisle. There was one thing her grandma appreciated and that was a well turned-out gentleman.

Christine and Jeff sat at their last planning session with the wedding planner. They'd opted for a buffet style meal due to the enormous amount of food allergies on both sides of their families. There were those who couldn't eat shellfish, those who wouldn't eat meat of any kind, and those who really just didn't care. In the end Jeff decided on prime rib, parsley potatoes, and eggplant parmesan- for a vegetarian selection- and chicken cordon bleu. The bar would be an open bar for the first three hours and after that the guests would be on their own. As for music they selected a DJ and a large dance floor. While Christine was sure her family would dance the night away, Jeff had his doubts where his family of librarians and school teachers were concerned.

As for the cake, Christine didn't know what all the fuss was about. They were having over one hundred fifty guests and would need three or four layers. They selected a tiered design, separated by columns. The outside of the cake would be decorated in rolled fondant with real roses and ivy. Jeff preferred carrot cake and Christine wanted yellow cake. In the end, Christine decided they should have both.

"I don't see why we have to choose. There are four layers- couldn't each be a different type of cake?"

The wedding planner nodded her head in affirmation.

"Okay- then let's do yellow cake on the bottom. Carrot on the next layer. Marble on the third layer. And chocolate on top."

"Sounds good to me."

"What about table arrangements?"

"Surprise us. Colours are platinum and off white."

"Okay. And linens?"

"Same thing. We're not worried about it."

"Okay. Centrepieces?"

"That's all you." Jeff winked at Christine.

"I'm not concerned about that either. I'm sure you'll come up with something suitable within the budget we gave you." Christine added.

"I have to say- you two are certainly different than the last time we met- more laid back."

"We've figured out what matters." Jeff squeezed Christine's hand.

"Okay. Then I guess we're all done here. I spoke with the

photographer and he will come see the venue next week. He does his

thing and I do mine. We'll coordinate important things like the

father-daughter dance, etc."

"Okay. We'll see you in a week or two."

Jeff and Christine stood to walk outside. The sun was bright

and warm. On their way across the car park, Christine stopped across

from a huge oak tree on the eighteenth hole of the golf course.

"I wonder if we could get a picture made here."

"I think that's a nice idea. With the golf course in the

background. You've got my vote."

Jeff hugged her goodbye at her car and headed back into

work for the rest of the afternoon. It was Christine's day off and she

still needed wedding shoes. She wanted something comfortable.

Height was never all that important to her, she was a shorty and she

was proud of it. Her roommate agreed to meet her at the largest mall

in the area and help her on her shoe quest. Christine jumped in her

car and drove carefully over to the mall. She waited outside for

Vanessa for over fifteen minutes. Nada. She checked her cell phone

and saw she didn't have any new messages. Then across the car park

she saw a silver haired lady she knew was her grandmother.

Christine walked over to greet her.

"Hey, Grandma. What's up?"

"I stopped by your house to bring you something for next week and Vanessa was there. She has a stomach virus so I offered to come shopping with you instead. Poor girl- she looked awful."

"Gosh- I hope I don't catch it."

"Me too. So she said something about shoe shopping and I still need a dress."

"Good. Hopefully we can get them both out of the way."

Christine led the way into the first department store. Grandma looked at the sequined dinner dresses and eventually ruled them out as *looking entirely too old* for her. Under her breath she was humming a song.

"What song are you humming?"

"Danny Boy."

"It's beautiful. Would you teach it to me?"

"Sure."

Right there, on the floor of the department store, her grandmother taught her all of the verses to *Danny Boy*. When she'd been a little girl Grandma would sing with her for hours. Anything from Patsy Cline to Big Band World War II hits. Some of her favourites were *I'll Walk Alone* and *Always.* While Grandma's high soprano was far prettier than her own alto voice, singing was something they enjoyed doing together. Christine never sang in public and probably wouldn't have even considered it six months earlier, but here she was now- in the middle of a department store belting out the verses to *Danny Boy.*

When they'd finished a few older women were clapping for them. Christine was sure her face was nearly as purple as the beaded suit now in her grandmother's left hand.

"I think it'll look nice, Grandma."

"Good. Let's go try it on."

They carried it into the dressing room where she helped her remove the top, skirt, and jacket from the hangers. Christine handed them over the top of the dressing room door and then waited patiently to see how it looked. When grandma opened the door, the suit looked stunning. It picked up the grey flecks surrounding her icy blue eyes. Christine found it remarkable how fit grandma was even now. Vanessa remarked on the same thing once before, claiming she hoped she looked that good when she hit forty, let alone any age beyond seventy.

"That's a keeper." Christine smiled.

"I think you're right. Now let's go see what we can do about these shoes of yours. Did you have anything particular in mind?" Grandma asked over the closed door as she handed the suit to Christine to hang back up.

"Nothing too high. I want to dance and I have to be comfortable. I certainly don't want to be tripping or falling."

"Smart, sensible girl. Let's go."

Grandma swung the door open. They walked out into the mall and passed several stores along the way. A jewellry store on the right seemed to catch Grandma's eye.

"Let's stop in here."

"Okay."

They walked over and shopped the cases. The gentleman behind the counter recognised Grandma immediately.

"So good to see you back, Kay . Let me get your item. I think you'll be pleased with how well it turned out."

He disappeared into the back room and reappeared with a gold necklace with some sort of pendent hanging from it. Kay stepped nearer to take it from him and get a better look. Now even Christine's curiosity was piqued. She stepped over and saw the object under scrutiny was her grandmother's very own basket scarf pin. It had been modified slightly and now could be worn as a pendent.

"It's striking as a pendent." Christine acknowledged.

"I'm glad you like it. Try it on."

Christine turned and Grandma clasped the necklace behind her back. Christine reached her hand up to touch it.

"It's lovely, Grandma."

"It's yours."

"But..."

"No arguments. I want you to have it and scarves are outdated. Your generation doesn't typically wear them anymore and in Florida you'll never get the chance. And it still comes off, if you want to wear it as a scarf pin, you just detach it like so."

Christine hugged her grandmother tightly.

"Thank you."

"Now open it and look inside."

Christine opened it and inside a pair of blue sapphires fell out into her hand.

"When I got it from your grandfather it held diamond star earrings. I've given you sapphires and someday when you give it to your daughter or granddaughter- you'll put something inside."

Christine and her grandmother shared tears and a silent embrace. Afterwards they strolled through the mall until they located the perfect pair of not too high pumps in a simple off white colour.

Later in the afternoon, Christine sat on the couch in her living room. She looked down and caught a glimpse of her new necklace. The pendent was beautiful. It had been cleaned and the gold sparkled in the light. In her ears she wore the sapphire earrings. Between the pendent and the earrings she'd covered old, new, borrowed and blue. She wasn't sure if the order was correct and knew it didn't matter. Her wedding day was only a week away. Tomorrow she'd sign the papers to vacate her apartment two weeks after her wedding. She and Jeff first planned on taking a honeymoon and when they returned she'd have four days to move her things into Jeff's house and clean out her apartment.

He owned quite nice furniture, but agreed to take her stuff as well. For the first few weeks they'd have enough to furnish two homes but in time she was sure they'd work it out. Her bedroom furniture would go in his guest bedroom which currently housed a not-so-comfortable futon. She gave her washer and dryer to Vanessa who was moving soon as well. She offered her the living room furniture but she didn't need it- her fiance had that covered already.

Over the next few days, Christine was busy between work and packing for her honeymoon. They were going to Rome and she wasn't sure what the weather would be like this time of year. According to the reports it could vary between warm and freezing in less than twenty-four hours. She decided in this case more was better and packed a bunch of just about everything. The days crept passed one by one and her wedding day finally arrived. She slept in until nine o'clock, at which point her sister and mother came pounding on her door. When she opened it, Christine saw even her grandmother was there with them.

"Come on. We have to get moving. We need to be at the spa in half an hour and it's a ways away."

"So early? The wedding's not until seven o'clock this evening."

"We are doing a spa day! Come on!"

Her sister was already in Christine's room choosing her clothes for the day. Christine sauntered in and pulled on a pair of jeans followed by some well worn flip flops.

"I didn't get to do this when I got married! Don't deny your grandmother this opportunity at happiness!" Grandma teased from the kitchen where she'd fixed herself a cup of coffee.

"Okay. I'm ready."

After this came a day filled with pampering. There were massages, manicures, pedicures, relaxing aroma therapy sessions, and calming facials. By the end of it, Christine wasn't sure if she should sleep or get dressed for her wedding. The last part was hair and make-up. A stylist was just finishing her grandmother's curled style, setting it in place with spray. Christine was next and she wanted it up and out of the way. A beautiful bun with cascading curls framing her face was her mom's suggestion and she'd been right. Lastly her sister pinned her veil in place.

Next, a cosmetologist set to work making them all gorgeous and when the finishing touches were done- the wedding party was ready. Christine had no idea what the men were up to but she hoped it was fun. Out of the corner of her eye she saw a spry woman enter the shop. A strong British brogue gave her away as no other than Edith. Christine shot to her feet.

"Surprise! We thought we'd surprise you."

It meant the world to Christine that her grandmother's only living brother and his wife flew all the way from England to be at her wedding. She couldn't believe it.

"Where's Anthony?"

"He's with the men- no doubt doing what he did the day of our wedding. Getting snockered."

"That's exactly what Ray did on the eve of our wedding."

Chapter Eighteen

Manchester, England

The eve before Kay's wedding to Ray.

Three of Kay's brothers arrived home the day before the wedding and she made each of them promise to be on his best behaviour. When they offered to take Ray out for a final prenuptial outing she was fearful if they'd even bring him home in one piece.

Ray arrived around midday, but he didn't arrive alone. Pee-Pee, Piggy, and Ronald were with him. Kay wondered about Dick's whereabouts but decided he probably wouldn't be present. She hadn't seen him since his falling out with Constance and coming now would hardly be appropriate. Hilda had taken Ray's measurements that Kay provided a few months earlier and had sewn him an amazing navy blue suit along with a pinstriped shirt. She did one final fitting at Harry's and he was ready for the next day's ceremony, but when he learned of Kay's dress not being completed he opted to wear his army uniform instead. He thought it would be best if he saved his new suit to wear back home with her finished dress. This won Hilda's stamp of approval. She offered to mail the suit to the States for him and he gladly accepted. Outside the rowdy mixture of G.I.'s and Kay's brothers awaited him. The lot of them presented him with a torpedo which read SADSACKS on one side in bold lettering. Kay figured it was some sort of male inside joke and decided she didn't want to know further details.

"Don't worry yourself, Katie. He's in good hands. You'll see him tomorrow at the church." Billy smiled.

"He better be in good form." She teased.

"Oh he will be! Several pints downed! Just don't get too close- he may stink!" Billy jested.

Kay gave them all a warning look. They marched Ray away amid cheers and whistles.

"What do you think they have in mind?" Kay asked

Constance.

"Probably better you don't know. Let's go."

"Where to?"

"Hilda's. She's planned you a shower."

Kay was greeted by smiles and hugs. All of her closest friends were there. Even Mary made the journey from Blackpool. After sipping tea and enjoying a delectable cake, she opened the few small packages awaiting her. From Hilda there was a beautiful apron in pale pink with eyelet lace trimming the bottom hemline. From Theresa and Veronica there was a sensible white satin nightgown with matching dressing gown. Finally, there was a gift from Constance. Kay looked at her, nearly afraid to open it.

Inside there was a red bra, matching panties and garter belt.

"Now you have something new to hold those silk stockings up!"

"Constance! Where did you get these?"

"I sent word to a friend in London along with some money. She's a dancer and knew just where to find such things."

Kay wasn't sure whether she'd ever actually wear the set but the kind gesture as well as the thought and expense which probably went into the gift were sweet. There was conversation, tea, and shortbread cookies. The afternoon was a splendid one and passed all too quickly. She thanked everyone as she and Constance left for the railway station sometime later. At home she washed and set her hair. She waited up for Ray as late as she could, but finally fell asleep around midnight. She was awakened by a riotous commotion coming from downstairs shortly before dawn. She stumbled to the stairs to find George and Jonathan lugging a plastered Ray up the stairs.

"He's sloshed!"

"Just a bit, sis."

"Where are you taking him?"

"Your room. Where else?"

They threw him across her bed and walked out laughing. Kay stood staring at his passed out form lying across her bed. He opened his eyes and extended his hand to her.

"Not on your life. Sleep it off, Ray."

She closed the door softly and went down to make breakfast. Hours later Ray appeared in the kitchen.

"You sore with me, Charlie?"

"Nope. I'm glad you enjoyed yourself. Are you sober enough

to walk down the aisle in a couple of hours?"

"Of course."

"Good. Get cleaned up. I'll see you at the church."

"Where are you going?"

"Constance's house to get ready."

He walked over and patted her on the butt. She smacked his hand away.

"Just warming you up a bit. I plan on touching a lot more than that tonight."

"Not if you've been drinking."

He leaned in and kissed her lightly before she left him standing in the kitchen. Constance, Theresa, and Mary helped Kay get into her suit. She'd opted to wear a robin's egg blue suit with thin white pinstripes. It zipped up the front and was tightly fitted across the chest. Along the pleated neckline there was simple piping. The skirt was an a-line skirt which hung to mid-calf. Theresa put the finishing touches on her make-up and hair. For jewellry she wore her pearl bracelet from Anthony along with her heart shaped locket and necklace from Ray. They walked the two blocks to the church. The church was already full, their guests seated on both sides of the centre aisle. Ray stood at the altar, the most handsome G.I. she'd ever seen. His hair was styled in sweeping curls with one long spiraled curl laying lazily on his forehead. The effects of a night's partying were not visible. Mary stood to the left of the altar, serving as her maid of honour.

Kay walked down the aisle escorted by George. Jonathan and Billy stood beside Ray at the altar. All of them dressed in their Sunday best. While they may have initially disapproved of her marrying a Yank they seemed to have warmed to him. When George gave her away he leaned in and lovingly kissed her cheek.

"Be happy, sis."

While her parents and Jimmy were not there, Kay was sure they were looking on from heaven's gates, smiling down on her this day. Anthony's presence was missed but out of all of her brothers he knew Ray the best. It was fitting since he'd already gotten to spend so much time with Ray, the others get a turn as well.

The Catholic wedding mass was a long one. By the time they had exchanged vows and Ray had kissed her sweetly, the small church had heated up significantly. Moments later they stepped outside into the cool afternoon air and said goodbye to their friends.

They made their way the short distance to the Registrar's Office, where they signed their marriage licence and filed it, making everything official. They were carried to the railway station where they caught a train to Morecambe by the Bay.

Kay had visited there once as a young child, but not since. When they arrived they checked into a beautiful hotel overlooking the bay. The cries of gulls and the smell of the tide greeted them. As the sunset on their wedding day, the war was quickly becoming a memory to her- replaced by the new happiness she found with Ray.

Epilogue

Christine stood at the doors to the church. The church bells chimed seven o'clock and she heard the music playing, signaling Carol and the best man, Eric, to walk down the aisle. Carol looked stunning today. Her silver dress breezily touched the floor, sweeping it with each step. She was tall and elegant. It was a running joke between them that she got all the height genes and Christine the short ones. She and Eric arrived at the altar turning to face the attendees. The wedding march began to play and Christine took a final deep breath.

Her father squeezed her arm and walked in time with her down the aisle. Her grandmother was seated in the very front row. Kay looked beautiful in the purple suit they'd chosen together. Around her neck hung her gold locket and on her wrist a delicate pearl bracelet. Her ring finger was adorned by the simple gold band Ray gave her during their second ceremony in the States. Christine couldn't remember ever seeing her without it.

At the altar, Christine's father lifted her veil and kissed her lightly on the cheek. Jeff stood across from her beaming. The mass was lengthy and the kneeling was complicated by her skirt and its bulk. In this moment she was thankful she hadn't chosen something tight and fitted. When the mass ended they walked out to the awaiting limo which carried them to their reception. There a tribute was made to her great aunt and uncle, Edith and Anthony, who'd been married for fifty years. Jeff and Christine danced until the last song was played and left in a shower of bubbles.

Marriage began anew- *they lived life...a wonderful, love filled life.*